ALSO BY ELIZA CLARK

Miss You Like Crazy
What You Need

Bite the Stars

Bite the Stars

a novel

Eliza Clark

Harper*Perennial*Canada
HarperCollins*PublishersLtd*

BITE THE STARS
Copyright © 1999 by Eliza Clark.
All rights reserved. No part of this book may be
used or reproduced in any manner whatsoever
without prior written permission except in the
case of brief quotations embodied in reviews.
For information address HarperCollins Publishers
Ltd, 55 Avenue Road, Suite 2900, Toronto,
Ontario, Canada M5R 3L2.

http://www.harpercanada.com

HarperCollins books may be purchased for
educational, business, or sales promotional use.
For information please write: Special Markets
Department, HarperCollins Canada, 55 Avenue
Road, Suite 2900, Toronto,
Ontario, Canada M5R 3L2.

First HarperFlamingo ed. ISBN 0-00-225512-X
First HarperPerennialCanada ed.
    ISBN 0-00-648111-6

Canadian Cataloguing in Publication Data

Clark, Eliza
Bite the stars

ISBN 0-00-648111-6

I. Title

PS8555.L355B57 2000 C813'.54 C99-932412-8
PR9199.3.C52B58 2000

00 01 02 03 04 RRD 8 7 6 5 4 3 2 1

Printed and bound in the United States

Out there you can kick up the dust, you can dance to fiddle music, watch the alfalfa bloom. There breathing's easy. Nights move faster. And you tell time by the clock. Go out there and bite the stars. For me.

— *Birdman of Alcatraz*

Bite the Stars

DOVES

Doves build flimsy nests of twigs. They lay one or two pale, unmarked eggs. Though similar to pigeons, doves tend to be more slender and graceful, with pointed rather than fan-shaped tails. Known for their gentle cooing calls, white doves are symbols of peace, despite by nature they are not pacifists, and will fight as required. In folklore, a white dove flying around a person or resting on his windowsill is an omen of death not far distant, but ensures peace to the departing soul. If white doves fly at the time of an execution, they promise not only peace to come, but love beyond, everlasting.

ONE

My son was born in a tornado. In a church crowded with Palm Sunday worshipers, the wind came on, banging and rattling the clapboards like the devil wanted in. Nineteen died in that little church I loved. Pretty young girls all dressed up, rustling in the front pews, waiting their turn at singing in the Easter pageant when the roof caved in on their heads. A man ran down the aisle yelling for us to get down, and then the lights went out. The wind was roaring at three hundred miles an hour, made you want to cover your ears, block its screaming. The woman right next to me was crushed flat. Outside in the old graveyard, tombstones were yanked from the jaw of the earth, broken like teeth smashed by a fist.

I used to keep a list of names in my Bible, a record of births and deaths in the community. In one minute a whole page was filled with all those little girls. I had to write their names down in black ink. Each one I wrote with care, fought to keep my hand steady, because at least their names should look fine written down forever, fine, pretty as their young faces were. I saw each of them clear as candles in a dark window as I spelled out the letters in their names. *Hannah*, I wrote, and the page blurred in front of me, a sweet child gone.

That day, tornadoes, hailstorms, and high winds whipped through Georgia and Tennessee, then in Charlotte, North Carolina a man got struck by lightning standing in his own front yard. A natural disaster. As if was anything natural about it.

My labor pains started two months early and my boy was born out of that whirlwind — three pounds, tiny as a shoe, and no sound at all. He made no sound. Quiet as the hush after an Amen shouted, but alive at least. My son, Cole James, I named after nobody I knew. Cole hates the story about the tornado and how he came to be born of it. I used to think it was because he felt so bad being sprung to life when all those others died. But that wasn't it. Hear me. Not those girls with their baby-high voices in our graceful, white church. No. Cole knew what it meant. He took their lives on his birthday, somehow, I don't know how. He stole their life spirit to pump his own into the world.

Cole is no good, and for a mama to say that, for a mama, I wish I could be dead. Used to be all I ever wanted was a child of my own. Used to be I felt lucky those years to have survived that storm, lucky and spared. But now I think about doom, what it is to be doomed. Cole is living proof ill winds blow in out of nowhere and stomp out love and mercy. But why that is? I gave years trying to figure it out and I guess there are years ahead of me to come. I won't ever let up wondering what went wrong.

Nobody thought a tornado would hit that morning. Because it was Easter maybe, or maybe because luck didn't seem far off. Things were peaceful all in all. I don't guess a soul thought disaster on their way to the hilltop church in the middle of farmlands and pine forests. I know I was just fussing in front of the mirror about how I looked in the only thing I could put on, seven months pregnant I carried straight out front, nothing fit me right. From the back I looked the same and I took to turning around and checking that familiar side of me, as opposed to the front which was too peculiar to judge. Not that I didn't like the shape in some ways, I was awed by it I think, my body being so set on growing a child it knew no bounds. But the thing about awe: a slice of it takes your breath. For just a split second, a cutting edge, air evades you, and then — wonder. You don't breathe because you don't have to, you don't need anything more. My worries weren't any bigger than that.

I guess there were signs, as always, when you check back for them. There'd been bad thunderstorms during the night. The air was still and silent that morning, so you couldn't care not to notice. The sky was muddy green, strange and swampy. The clouds hung low and threatening. And the birds. They'd all come from out of the trees and were sitting on the ground. That was something to see. I remember I stood a long time looking up at the eerie green sky and the birds huddled into themselves on the ground. I think I marveled at the way nature will always surprise you. I didn't know better than to see it as "everything is beautiful in its own way," as the song we sometimes sang in church went. I touched my belly and wished the baby could see the earth blooming with birds, flowers that any moment might spread wings, and fly.

Inside, the little church was more crowded than usual since the occasion was Palm Sunday, or Passion Sunday as it can be known. *Passion* meaning the suffering and death of Christ. We sang hymns to Jesus as king even while the lights flickered on and off because of the wind that all sudden rose out of nowhere and churned earth and sky together. We carried on despite it. The children in their bright party dresses waited to put on their play, *Watch the Lamb*. I found out after, the National Weather Service had issued a tornado watch for the area. Later there was a warning that a funnel cloud had been spotted dropping to the ground about the time the roof caved in. We didn't hear. I don't think anybody knew. Or if some members of the congregation ate breakfast with the radio on or the television, they didn't pay mind. Tornadoes are a fact of life in the spring in the Southeast. Doesn't matter now.

Can't anyone predict when a twister will roil into your life, I learned that the hard way. It'll come at you roaring like a freight train, ready or not. In China, thirteen schoolchildren were sucked up into a tornado and carried for twelve miles before being dropped gently to the ground, unhurt except for some cuts. A man was trapped inside his car when a tornado slammed into him, rocking the car violently and whirling it in circles. The man tried to hold onto his wife who was beside him but the suction pulled her through the window, and she was gone. In fifteen seconds he'd lost her and the sun shone mockingly from a blue heaven. That fast. Her body was found in a treetop in the next county, naked and hardly cradled. A twister will lift frogs and fish from ponds then let go of them over towns, showering a joke from the sky. It'll rain fish.

It got dark as night outside the church, an ugly purple and black. Thunder clashed and hailstones pelted the ground, winds pounded and shook the walls, monster hands rattled the doors on their hinges. Wood splintered. I looked around and saw faces gone pale, brows perspiring, hands holding the hymn-books tighter, children looking to their parents who gave them thin smiles then cast their eyes down and kept on singing. During "Wings of a Dove" the lights went out. *On the wings of a snow white dove, He sends His pure sweet love.* It was on us.

Debris started hitting the side of the church, something gray hit the window then a tree trunk came through. The wind roared like a squadron of jet fighters. Somebody yelled to get down on the floor. Those who could, fell, pushed under pews.

But there wasn't time. The whole building quaked on its foundation. I felt my hair and clothes being pulled up, the pressure popped my ears. The windows exploded blue and violet stained-glass shards. Pieces of trees and houses lashed in, deadly in their own right, with dirt and rain. Flying wood and metal whizzed like bullets in the air. The shoes were sucked off my feet and I prayed hard to be spared, myself and the child inside me. I was on the ground and I tucked into myself, like the birds, I covered my stomach with my wings, feathery wings, the wings of a snow white dove. *Lord.*

The roof lifted then collapsed. The walls buckled onto the children, the little girls, and others trapped under the pews. Sixteen died instantly, three later on. The minister's five-year-old daughter whose name was Hannah. I remember when she took her first steps, ran up to her mama while she was preaching at the altar and how we all clapped. Ruth Kay, the librarian, beside me. I patted Ruth's hand as if to reassure her it would be alright. I just patted her hand. Her husband Dale was at home with his brother who was there visiting because he'd just lost his wife to cancer. Now they'd both lost wives, were widowed. Poor Dale didn't even know it yet, he wasn't anyone's husband anymore. They were back to being brothers, two grown men, back where they started.

The wind was gone. I heard crying and whimpers but it was still, no raging wind. Near me a mother leaned over her child. She was covered in the girl's blood. I saw her put her arms under the girl's head, saw its dead weight, watched the mother bend to try and save her daughter by forcing her own breath into the child's lungs. Again and again she put her mouth on her daughter's and breathed. Willing life. The girl had bled badly. With every breath the mother put into her, she was further gone. I saw the mother's back shaking with sobs. She bent again. Finally the woman laid her head on her daughter's chest, on her pretty party dress. She laid her head on the girl's chest, I thought listening for a heartbeat, but she stayed that way. Suffering each breath of her own as unfair.

Maybe it was just the day before they'd gone shopping to find an Easter dress for the girl to wear to the church pageant. Maybe she'd tried on a bunch, her mother squeezed into the fitting room with her until they agreed on the perfect one. The girl was swinging the bag as they left the store hand in hand, maybe planning a hairstyle that would be nice? The shopping bag was still laying on the bedroom floor, maybe it would stay there a long time before the mother picked it up and threw it away.

My feet were cut up, my head pounded, but I walked out on my own. Two-hundred-year-old oaks had been snapped in half, sheets of tin roof were wrapped around branches like foil. Cars from the parking lot had been shuffled like cards in a deck, lifted and moved by the twister. A car was thrown on top of the church sign. A dusty blue car. Ambulances waited while rescue workers dug through the rubble and carried the injured out on broken pews.

No point to the word *why*, though it was on everybody's tongue. Why for a natural disaster was there nothing natural about it? You were not supposed to die in church, not in His house, not under the eye of God. You were supposed to be safe there, safer than anywhere else, sheltered from the storm. You were not supposed to die while you were singing praise to Jesus. Did He look away? Did He blink? That was the first time I questioned nature, questioned what was *natural*. I questioned my faith. It makes sense that nature would have its own laws and you could figure them out. But maybe not, maybe every-thing was always in flux.

Somebody nailed together a raggedy cross out of scrap, went and stood it in the middle of the fallen bricks and wood. Right away they did that, in the chaos, everybody running around. I looked long and hard at the cross, bold as it was, not even tilting to one side or the other but standing straight, straight in the midst of the wreckage. Could be nature was outside of God's laws, its crimes its own. Maybe God wasn't to blame. I guess for some, I wasn't sure about me yet, faith could be shaken, shaken to the core, but maybe not so easily lost.

I was almost at my car, what I wanted, all I wanted then, was just to go home. That's when I felt the first clenching pain, stopped me cold, my hand pressing my belly. Then slowly it eased and faded enough so I could walk on. I got to the car and leaned against the side, resting my weight on my bent arms. I saw that blood had drawn up beneath the skin of my arms and my legs as if I'd been pinched, blood drawn to the surface as though the tornado had reached inside me and tried to suck the life out through my pores. Someone behind me called to ask was I alright, and I waved that I was. Everybody had enough to concern themselves with. I eased myself into the car, turned the key in the ignition. The cramping pains came in deep waves, rolling in from far off and breaking hard then washing out to nothing again for a while. I drove believing if I could get home, put my feet up and rest, I'd keep the baby from coming. I believed that with my might. I drove with one hand on my stomach, biting my lip.

The car radio had bad static but I heard the news, the name of my little church being broadcast far and wide because tragedy had struck. Strange to hear our private suffering announced as a fact of history even while I saw the flashing red lights shrinking in the rearview mirror. Tornadoes had ripped through other parts of Tennessee, Georgia, and Alabama tearing up houses, knocking down trees, and swamping emergency rooms with the injured.

That night the skies were lit by lightning and a nearly full moon. In one minute, I counted a hundred flashes of lightning. My water broke and I couldn't pretend labor wasn't on me. There was no going back. From then my body took over and I let my mind slink into a dull corner of myself. I had to let it be. I was afraid. I had nobody I could call to be with me, nobody I wanted right then except Jackson, Cole's daddy, and he wasn't mine, he didn't belong to me. I'd have this baby by myself and I'd raise it by myself. Then I'd have part of what I always wanted. There are all kinds of ways to be lonely, with or without company, or the man you love.

I packed my comb and toothbrush, socks, I don't know what all, things I thought I would need. I hadn't planned this far ahead, didn't expect to have to. Times I'd be bent double breathing hard. I moved around packing a newborn sleeper, buttercup yellow. In the store the sleeper had seemed smaller than real, sized zero to three months, like to have fit a doll. Size zero. But now this was less than that. This was less than zero. I put my face in my hands. I don't think I ever felt so lonely before. But then I told myself this was what I wanted, this baby, and I looked down at my belly and I had to be strong and I knew of course I wasn't alone. I was somebody's mama already. I prayed, shaken faith or not. *Please let my baby live. I don't care how tiny he is or how big that sleeper will be on him. Let him live.*

I was shaking hard, my jaw ached from my teeth chattering. I drove to the hospital, slow when I had to, fast when I could. I thought I would split apart, the pain was jagged. I heard wailing, far off down the corridor, another woman like me. But I chewed my lip to keep quiet. I didn't want my baby to hear me screaming, not when he was new in the world or any time after.

I remember someone held my hand, some kind nurse let me hold of her hand. Forceps to guard the baby's skull. I did my best to push through the pain, trying to get beyond to the calm that had to be on the other side. I would have given up. But there was no choice — the stark truth hit me. I wasn't the one who mattered anymore, surely as I wasn't alone, I didn't matter near as much as my baby, I wasn't as important. I would have died in a flash for him, stepped in front of a train, dove off a mountaintop. I would, willingly, have forsaken myself. *Let him live.* In that way nothing ever would be the same, and it was both sweet and bitter to swallow. But it just came on me, as ferocious a belief as I've ever had or would have. My baby mattered more than I did.

I gave birth to Cole while thunderstorms raged and lightning lit the curtained windows. He was a strong baby for one so tiny and fought to take the help he was given. He was too early to breathe on his own although he had a steady heartbeat. Because he was premature, he had to be kept in an incubator at first. The sterile glass box was like Snow White's coffin in the woods, would he wake from the spell or sleep on endlessly? The temperature and the oxygen supply inside the incubator were controlled and he was fed through a tube passed down his nose into his stomach. I couldn't take my eyes off him, that little stranger, my son. So young a baby can't fight infection and the nurses handled him only when they had to. He was scarcely held. I couldn't touch him at all. Later, I was able to but stroke him light as a feather along his clear skin, whether he felt it or not who knows, and I had to wear a glove.

Nights I was haunted by the tornado. I'd dream a solid black cloud, a long narrow funnel dropping from it, sky connected to earth by a wavering umbilical cord. Luminous, the churning funnel would stretch downward in silence, then, tentative almost, it would bend gracefully and point to the church on the hill where we'd congregated. It seemed to me the finger of God, and it shimmered with power. Palm Sunday. The day Jesus entered Jerusalem and was acclaimed king by the same crowd that would all too soon demand his death. Cole was born from devastation, a brand new light in the darkness. Who dreamed he was darkness? The light he was to me, radiant energy my eyes were moved by.

I didn't leave the incubator. I pressed my hand on the hard glass lid and the warmth from my palm left a mark that disappeared into thin air. I watched his small back rising and falling as he drew breaths. He was on his own from before he should even have been born. I stood by him. I touched the glass and sang hushed lullaby songs. When I'm in the prison now, I can't help but think of that early time. I'm still talking to my son through a wall of glass.

Cole is at Riverbend in Nashville, a maximum-security institution, unit 2, inmates under sentence of death. In less than a week now, the same sun will rise over me that will rise over Cole, and then it will set on me alone. It's unnatural. I never thought, never intended to outlive my child. How will I? Our last real hope is to plead with the Governor for clemency, ask him to commute Cole's sentence to life. After all these years, courts and appeals and judges, it's my voice left. My words to the one man who can save him. Save him on earth. Are there words? I am his mother, I brought him into this world. Can I say what needs to be said, let him live?

I remember standing by the incubator looking at my newborn baby, feeling useless. I tried pumping breast milk to give to him but it didn't work out. I'd stand in the shower under the hot rain of water and massage my breasts until they let down and the milk came. There just wasn't enough. Maybe you need your baby like it needs you. I could have filled bottles with my tears. I should have tried harder to fight the emptiness — no infant in my arms. I could hardly stand not holding him. I'd watch Cole's little ruby lips sucking in his sleep and my chest ached even as the milk dried up.

Maybe once back then we could have each done the other good. It must be a powerful feeling to nurture your baby from your own body. I've thought I might have given Cole some of my immunities, hard-won defenses that would have kept him safe from harm. Premature babies don't have body fat and they can't store heat. It all goes out through their heads and their hands. Cole wore a pale blue bonnet the size of an orange and mittens knit in soft cotton wool by a senior, then donated to the maternity ward. I was so thankful someone had taken the time, had troubled to keep my baby warm and protected. He needed so much, I was scared how to give it to him.

TWO

The first few weeks and months caring for my baby boy were a blissful haze. I didn't have a thought in my head, just a fine full satisfaction. I was content to be peaceful. The hours of the days ran into each other and lost their required meaning. We were the center of our own universe. I'd give Cole a bottle and rock him till he fell asleep, then lay on the bed holding his solid new weight against me, growing heavier and heavier. I wanted nothing else. In his face was fragile perfection, and contained beneath the gentle swell of his skull, all his possibilities. I looked at each part of him as a precious victory. I would rest with my lips against his soft round head and marvel at my potent love.

Sometimes we'd sleep and dream together, even babies dream, but more often my eyes stayed wide open. I didn't want to miss anything. His sigh, a yawn. I was hungry for him, pangs that almost hurt they were so strong, so deep. When I dreamed, it was visions of fear. I dreamed I was in a burning building, flaming candles in my hair. I was crying *Fire! Fire!* but I couldn't make the sound out loud. Through a distant window, I could see the blue ocean. There was a door covered in charred and peeling wallpaper. The smoke was choking me. I held my arms out in front like a sleepwalker witching my way towards the door. The blue ocean would save me. As I was about to pull the door handle, a baby's faint cry. My baby. But where in the burning house, and why hadn't I remembered him before? I turned to climb a staircase that wound up and up. The boards broke, splintering beneath me, and I couldn't say how far I'd get.

Mama died of cancer just after I found out I was pregnant with Cole, she never knew about it, and left me her house, all the crumbling flea-market antiques she collected. Sets of china, old linens, silverware. One night I sat on the veranda in a weathered wicker chaise, hoping for the slightest breeze. Cole was lying in a baby basket at my feet, his wispy hair damp on his brow, nothing on save a diaper. Sometimes I could nap out there when I couldn't get to sleep inside. Like Cole would later, find calm in the fresh air, space enough to relax under the moon beaming through a clutch of pines. He had his thumb in his mouth, pulling on it now and then. His eyelids fell closed and I tiptoed into the house for the mosquito netting. I draped it over his basket and tucked it in tight along the edges.

My mind went to Jackson the way it did when I was too on my own to be held back by pride. I heard the crickets singing in the grass. I saw Jackson, undoing my dress a slow button at a time. He called my name, called it under his breath in a husky voice that made me tremble. I saw his eyes, closing. Desire tugged, a deep flip low in my belly. All the yearning I did wondering when or if he'd show his face at my door. Come and see what we made together. It was an ache I lived with.

In the early morning light, I loosed the netting and folded it back from the basket. My knees went weak. I pressed my palm to my lips to stop from crying out. Cole was covered head to toe in mosquito bites, swollen into mean scarlet welts. I'd caught the bugs in with him, trapped them beneath the fine mesh. He cooed at me the way he did always when he woke, happy to see me. I picked him up, my baby. Held him against me, sorry rocking us both.

As he grew, sometimes I'd think I could see right into his head, I knew him. Other times I didn't have a clue. When he was born, he was a miracle. To me he was. New life born out of all that sorrow and destruction. I watched him from the outside. Way he was. I couldn't hear the thoughts in his head or feel the blood run in rivers in his veins. Strange. He was my child. I thought I ought to know who he was inside.

We both made mistakes, could hurt each other without trying. Cole could never touch a thing. If he ever got close enough to reach out to touch the thing he admired, whatever it was, he'd wreck it. Cole ruined everything he yearned to hold. It twisted him and almost ended us both.

Most everything I've ever known, know to this day, I read it in a book. Books have been my salvation since I was a child. If I could read every hour from sunrise to sundown, I would. Gladly I would. I used to buy books at yard sales, sometimes I'd get a whole box for a dollar. I chose them by how pretty they were, if they had flowers or a nice pattern on their spines I picked them up. I always had an armful of books to take home and read. Then after a while, I came to notice the names of the authors who wrote the books. Came to recognize some I liked and I looked for those especially. I had a collection of good books by writers I wasn't the only one to admire. They were classics, old classics and modern classics, some were classics to me. I was proud of how many books I had, that I'd read all of them. I learned more on my own that way than I did through to the end of high school. I used to wish I could have gone on to college but then, when that couldn't happen, I just told myself, there are the books, girl, what do you want to know? They were precious to me.

My bedroom was piled with books, lined in neat rows on shelves and heaped in stacks on the floor. It was them, not my bed, made that room a sanctuary for me. Didn't matter the weather outside, rain or shine, it just fell away and I lived in the book's world. One time, Cole went and closed himself in my bedroom without me knowing. He was mad because I'd denied him something, maybe I'd said no to giving him candy, he was just small. I thought he'd gone to his own room, it was quiet for a while, then I heard banging and went to check what he was doing.

I opened my bedroom door, found him standing in the middle of the room ruined books strewn everywhere. He'd ripped the pages out of my books. I couldn't move, stood struck in the doorway. Cole had frozen where he was too. All those books thrown around, not even one he hadn't got his hands on and wrecked some way. He never flinched his gaze off me, ripped a thick fistful of pages out of a book and flung them up into the air over his head. I shut my eyes, maybe I even put my hands over my eyes. But it didn't matter, I saw him still, cold look he had on his face. I opened my eyes to see white pages floating down like snowflakes. That's how cold it was. Cold enough for snow.

I wanted to hit him. I lunged towards him and he stepped back, covered his face with his arm as if to fend off a blow, even though I'd never struck him before. And I didn't then. I fell to my knees and started picking up the pages, bunching them to my chest. I guess somewhere in my mind I had a thought to tape them back in place, fix each book the way it was. Cole still didn't move. I looked up and he was watching me. I couldn't read him, his expression. His eyes were on the papers in my arms. I found a voice, asked him, "Why? Why my books?"

He shrugged his shoulders.

I could feel the anger rise in my throat. "That's not an answer," I said, as even as I could.

"I don't know," he mumbled.

The sight of him made me furious, I felt tears of frustration well in my eyes. I gathered up more pages off the floor, pages and pages I held to me. Finally I said, "What got into you? Something did."

"I don't know."

"That all you can say? You don't know much."

"I was mad."

"Why?"

"I don't know."

"Well, now we're both mad," I said. His face was blank. "I'm mad as hell. Madder than that." It was like talking to a statue, I shook my head. "Don't you care?"

His gaze left me and drifted over the tatters of books he'd flung everywhere.

"Don't you want to be good?" I said.

Then as if he was stone coming to life, he slowly reached down and picked up a piece of paper that was laying near him. He tried to smooth the creases out of it by rubbing it against his leg. He held it towards me and when I took it from him, he ran out of the room. It was a page of poetry. I read it to myself line by line. There was an island somewhere, far off.

I sat on the bedroom floor until after it was dark outside the window. I read loose pages and put them in piles. The books were mostly damaged past fixing. I wanted to memorize as much as I could. Save it inside my head, at least. Eventually Cole came back and stood over me. "I'm hungry," he said.

I shrugged, and a frown skimmed his face, then he left the room again. A while later he was back with a toy car and played driving it over the books, cutting roads through the mess, his mouth moving silently with the game he was playing in his head, the throb of the engine, rev of destruction.

I watched him and it was like nothing had happened, he wasn't troubled by guilt. He didn't seem to be. If he was sorry, I think it was only because he was hungry and he didn't want to be sitting so long in the darkening room. I bet he wondered why didn't I just get up and fix him something to eat? He was sorry about that. He climbed onto my lap, sped the car up and down my arm like it was a highway, part of his game only, an easy strip of flesh to drive over.

I got rid of my books, had to put them out for trash. It hurt to do it. I carried the boxes to the edge of the road for the truck to pick up, and as I set them down, I wondered what having Cole for my son would cost me. If I couldn't save my books, what could I save of myself? I thought about the cost of love. How you paid any price, the cost didn't matter, you loved at any cost. But then if the cost was too high — it took every- thing — if there was nothing left, could there still *be* love?

Cole couldn't help himself it seemed. Not that's an excuse, but the way he was cost him too. If I suffered, I have no doubt he suffered more. Cole rescued a bluebird out in the yard hurt with a broken wing. He stroked it so hard, patted it in love, caught it to his breast so tight, the poor bird suffocated. I can still hear him sobbing, "I killed it, Mama. I killed my pet." You can love a thing to death. With its last breath, you might know to let up the pressure and still not do it. That's how Cole was. All I could do was watch him, see what a mother is let see, what she can see, given the limited scope of her vision. I watched my son as best I could.

Later Cole's friend died in his arms almost the same way the bluebird had, except this time it wasn't all Cole's fault. Some of it was, though, and he knew it. He was different after that. Jess took a knife in his lung that had been meant for Cole. Cole's name was on the blade just he never got to read it. Jess was his best friend, a hero to him and a martyr, all at once. It was the last time I ever saw Cole cry, at the funeral, no matter how bad things got from then. When Jess's mother threw herself into the ground on top of her boy's casket, it was Cole who pulled her out. There at the grave was the last time I saw Cole cry in the daylight hours, though at night he cried plenty. Oceans in his sleep. He had nightmares that shook and tossed him till he clawed to wake, drenched in sweat, his heart pounding, eyes wide with fear. My son.

It's been years since I've touched Cole's face or even his sleeve, always separated during visits by a pane of thick glass. A glass wall between us, me on one side, him on the other. He comes into the cubicle, hardly a room, with his hands cuffed behind his back and they lock him inside it. There are bars on his door that are not on mine. He pushes his hands out through the pie flap and they uncuff him that way. Only then does he raise his head and give me a care. Only then does he smile, a movement of his mouth there and gone. I could feel his breath we're so close when we sit down, but I can't. Could if it weren't for the see-through glass wall, the broken laws, the mother and son we are, cut adrift long ago but still sooner than time.

"How are you?" I ask him.

He shrugs.

He won't worry me by telling me how he is. But I can see. We each try to be brave. We lean on that. But I can see his clothes hang off him, his bones near the surface of his pale skin, white-hard through the flesh. I will never get used to him being right there. Right there and I can't hold him. That little scar he has just below his eye. How did he get that? I think back but I don't remember. I want to kiss it. He flattens his hand to the glass wall between us and I press mine back in response, as ever it feels lifeless cold.

Riverbend's Public Information Officer has given me the facts about the lethal injection procedure. This is so I can be prepared for what will happen. She tells me I need to be ready for it. I hear her voice and I wonder if she is a mother herself. I wonder how many mothers she has told this to. Her voice is controlled despite she's talking about killing my boy. How do you prepare, be ready?

There is a witness room and a death chamber. A gurney with six leather straps. Arms are extended and wrists bound in place. The table is in the shape of a cross. The execution technician, who is not a doctor or nurse because the AMA's Code of Ethics forbids medical professionals from taking part in executions, will insert an IV into the forearm after swabbing the area first with alcohol. I ask her if this is to prevent infection? She pauses. I wait. I do not let my eyes waver off hers. I want her to look away from me, be shamed. But she doesn't even blink. She tells me I ought to be glad the procedure is clean and as antiseptic as it is, no hospital room is more hygienic.

I have lost my voice. If I could, I would tell her that this is all wrong. It is not a clean thing to do, no matter how morally sparkling it seems to her. It should be terrible, witnessed in the light of day, not shrouded in darkness and secrecy after midnight. It should be done in public so people can see what's going on, the full horror. A man being killed. Some mother's son. It shouldn't be easy, sanitized. But I don't say any of that, because she's right. This is my child, grown as he is, and I don't want him to suffer. I don't want a show made out of him. I want dignity. I want him to be in a pure white room, a room so shiny and dazzling white that when he closes his eyes it's like he's looking full into the sun. He will be warmed by it.

I clear my throat. "If you stare into the sun," I tell her, "you'll be blinded by white light. The light of merciful angels."

"Are you okay?" she asks. "I know this takes a toll."

I wonder how other mothers fare. Do they scream or faint or hit her? I watch her mouth, the way she shapes each word, they pierce me like invisible arrows, leave wounds that don't show.

The warden will give the signal and a mixture of sodium pentothal to render unconsciousness, pancuronium bromide to paralyze the diaphragm and stop the breathing, and potassium chloride to stop the heartbeat will flow through the IV line. The mixture costs $71.50. Did I hear her right? I think about the poison running through Cole's veins where our shared blood is, my blood and Jackson's blood, all our combined history. $71.50. Maybe she means to prove the death penalty isn't costly to taxpayers? Death comes in about two minutes. The cost, when I try to add it up, comes out different for me.

In Texas, she confides, where they made their own lethal injection machine, it takes almost eighteen minutes to die because between each chemical they have to flush saline through the line so the acid and alkaline solutions don't react by crystallizing and backing up. I can tell she thinks this will comfort me, she believes faster is better, more merciful. But again her math is messed up. She hasn't counted the seven years spent killing time on the row. Time's been in no hurry and now it wants to run out.

My son, Cole James, was born in a tornado. The sky was black and children died waiting to sing praises to heaven. The wind tore trees from the earth and whirled their useless roots through the air. Roots that lost their hold, their grip on history and place.

Every month or so a man at Riverbend is taken from his cell and executed during the night "at any time before the hour of sunrise" as decreed by the statute. Anti-death-penalty protesters gather outside the coiled razor-wire fences in candlelight with their pots, pans, and wooden flutes as the official witnesses file inside. The coils are spun like funnel clouds, it seems to my eye. When the time comes, the warden will nod to the executioner, an unknown man or woman, or both, in the room next to the death chamber. There will be a sudden deep breath, a chin stiffened upward, and then nothing. Not a cry or flutter of a raised finger. I will stand if my knees let me.

MOSQUITOES

Flying adults emerge in spring within days of the blooming of chokecherry trees. They feed on the sweet nectar of flowering trees and shrubs, and honeydew excreted by insects that suck plant juices. After they are satiated on nectar, both sexes mate several times. Males use their bushy antennae to detect the distinct buzz of female wingbeats. Only females need blood, males don't bite. The razor-thin stylet within the long proboscis pierces the flesh and the sucking tube is inserted into a tiny blood vessel. Saliva containing an anticoagulant to keep the blood flowing is injected into the wound. They feed until their abdomens balloon red with blood.

THREE

Cole dropped out of high school when he was sixteen and moved out right after, wandered around getting into trouble. He went through a mooning phase. I'd be in Wal-Mart or Taco Bell and see Cole mooning random targets. I can't tell how often I stood mortified while he waggled his smooth round butt at some stranger passing him by. That was nothing. He got guns and flashed them at strangers too, while he robbed them of their wallets and jewelry. He got caught often enough I knew what was going on. So many nights I'd laid in my bed worrying about him. Used to be, when he was small, I worried about myself. I used to think, what if I became ill and couldn't care for him, what if I was ill already? I'd lay there, full of dread, so anxious I couldn't close my eyes to sleep, picturing disease eating its way through my body. Taking me, slowly but surely, from my son. He'd be left alone when I died. The thought crushed me, I felt the weight of it on my chest. He needed me and I needed him back.

When I was pregnant, I remember laying in the dark with my hands on my swollen belly waiting to feel the life move beneath them. My body felt vast as the ocean, rolling with tides. When Cole was tiny, I'd touch the soft spot on his head with wonder, so absolutely fragile I'd do anything to protect it. Nights after he left, I'd take out his baby pictures and study them like bones I'd dug up. How much was my fault? I'd go over and over mistakes I'd made, replay bad calls, lapses in judgment, any slight that might have been hurtful to a little boy. Cole was a wound I wouldn't let heal. I'd fall asleep, the tears still wet on my temples, my mind racing and sorry for him, the wild wind he'd been born out of and had become. Dangerous and storming, hail-fury.

My sister raised Cole from the time he was two until he turned five. Ellen offered to take Cole so I could work nights at the hospital where I laundered the linens, make some money, fix up the house so it was a better place to live. She'd raise him in a family. So many things went into that happening, the way she was and I was, all our lives. Way I saw myself, I guess. Ellen had the luxury of more comfortable means than I did. It wasn't unheard of for children to be reared by other than blood-parents, by hands of sisters or aunts or bachelor uncles. It was almost tradition in some big old families. The natural parents worked so hard that they were spent at the end of the day, wrung dry, with nothing left over inside them to nurture a child. It was thought the children would get more love somewhere else. But being tired and being out of love aren't the same thing. My boy wouldn't have gone loveless. I don't know how I made it three years without him. I saw him, but he wasn't mine. Three years and I honestly thought it was best. I tried to grow up and act sensible. I was twenty-six, which sounds old enough in years, but I wasn't mature. I think now though a child should be with his mama almost no matter what. A mama is vital, despite everything. You are what you are and kids will turn the other cheek so often you can but shake your head in wonderment and pure gratitude. Sometimes they will — look at you and see only good.

My little boy came back sullen, with a heavy-browed stare, five years old and holding his hands in fists everywhere he went like that was natural for a child. He was so mad at me. I can hear myself. All the times I told him he was special to be born out of all that destruction, like a prize, I poisoned something. Cole never thought he was special, he thought the opposite. I bet he did. Why should he deserve to live when all those little girls died? He must have felt awful. Took me a long time to realize that.

Cole never had a daddy. Well he did of course, but a man's body is not a father. Cole never knew a father's love in my house, no man's arms to hold him or throw a ball to catch. My sister had two boys eight and ten, and a husband with a steady job though it kept him away a lot. Ellen used to come over and notice right away things I was doing wrong with Cole. He'd have a fever and I wouldn't know it. *This child is sick. He's burning up. What are you feeding him?* Be eating grapes she said he could choke on. *Don't you know those grapes'll lodge in his windpipe?* I started to wonder what was wrong with me, how unfit I was to be this baby's mama. One day Ellen came over while Cole was playing with a little plastic pork chop he'd picked up in the yard. I'd brought it inside and washed it off for him. *What's he got in his hand? That's a dog's toy.* Ellen said it was a toy made for a dog not a baby. The way she said it, for a dog. *Next thing you'll be giving him a bone.* I put my face in my hands. *Well, don't cry.*

Ellen had a way, she always did, made me feel I knew less than her. Was less than her. As kids, she wasn't shy like I was, she had all kinds of friends to play with. I had some too, and I had my books mostly, but my sister was my best friend, and Mama was. Ellen was older than me by nearly four years, though seemed to me sometimes she had the wisdom of the ages.

I remember Daddy brought us home a puppy once. He worked as a janitor at a veterinarian's office, and on occasion, once in a blue moon maybe, he'd take us after hours to pat the dogs that weren't too sick and give them milk biscuits from a box kept on a shelf beside their cages. He brought us home a little brown spotted puppy with blue eyes like sapphires. The color of Frank Sinatra's, Mama said. I'd dress the dog in doll clothes even though he chewed them off right away, and made him my inseparable playmate. I was the teacher and he was my student when we played school. I taught him the letters of the entire alphabet with my utmost patience and care. Then I wrote out simple words for him, showed him pictures of things like a chair, and I'd say, "Sit, boy. Chair." He liked school. He'd wag his tail so hard his behind almost left the ground.

I was teaching him to swim in the creek that used to be behind the house, before the water all dried up and grass overgrew it. I'd call for the puppy to follow me and we'd both dog-paddle. I had us swimming from one side to the other, back and forth shore to shore, ever calling him to keep up, because he needed the practice. If he didn't hear the sound of my voice urging him, he'd kind of slow so he was moving but in tiny half-circles, treading water getting nowhere.

Ellen came out of the house to tell me supper was ready on the table and I better come inside. She stood with her hands on her hips looking at the puppy doing his dog-paddle behind me. *He's just a baby still, Grace. He's too little for all that.*

I glanced back through my wet eyelashes that made everything sparkle, could see his pink tongue in his open mouth and he looked alright to me, looked like he was having fun. Ellen stood there a bit longer then went back in the house, not letting the screen door slam shut like I always did. I never remembered to close it gently. I think we did two maybe three more laps before

I climbed out onto the bank and wrapped my towel around me. The puppy was floating on the water then I saw him go under. I waded in and felt for him, carried him out.

Ellen slapped my face. *I told you.* She went to get a shoebox from her closet, line it with something soft, a piece of old flannel nightdress to lay the puppy on for his final rest. *You should've known better. You wore him out.* My cheek stung, I deserved it. But in my mind's eye still, when I saw the puppy panting to try to swim beside me, his paws pedaling the water, he looked like he was smiling. To me he looked cute and happy. I didn't know better. I looked with my eyes open and I didn't see right. I didn't see what Ellen saw at all, couldn't trust myself. Ellen took the shoebox and went off to bury him. She dressed all in black and cut a branch of Mama's sweetheart roses. I didn't deserve to be at the funeral but I would've gone if she'd let me.

I sat on my mama's lap in the living room and cried. I cried so long my daddy took his keys and drove off to a bar. I remember Mama's eyes watching him go. She rocked me and did what she always did when I was upset. She pointed to a place on the wall and said, "Look, child, you see that?"

The wallpaper was faded red and white, with Chinese scenes patterned on it. She'd tell me stories about what was going on in each one. About the strangely beautiful pagodas with roof upon roof, flowering trees that were airy as clouds, wise old men wearing flowing robes and long flowing beards, the exquisite birds and butterflies. As she spoke, it was so real to me it felt as if I was entering another world. I could see over the rolling hills where the sun was setting, lose myself there, small against the painted sky. I could rest far from my troubles, so far away I knew you'd have to dig and dig, deep down in the ground all the way out to the other side. The other side of the world where trees were wispy dreams. It always gave me comfort. Once or twice I tried to sit Cole on my lap, hold him still long enough to tell him those same stories living on the wallpaper from my childhood. He'd look but his eyes never fixed anywhere. He roamed the landscape but neither the birds nor the butterflies moved him. Strange how two people can look at the same thing and see something else.

The romance of faraway places always charmed me though I never did wander far from home. I was lucky that the house I was born in, that Mama left me and Cole came up in, satisfied my heart as a place to be. To some it might have seemed shabby, a rambling two-storied structure painted blue once, but the paint so peeling and cracked it was mostly gray now, to me had a simple elegance of line I found graceful. The windows were hung with lace panels of peacocks in full feather, or bowls of fruit and roses, that blew in the breeze. You might be born in the mountains, or out on the prairies, or at sea, but it doesn't mean your soul won't long for some other place. A place that will answer some need in you, some memory of belonging from back before mothers, before fathers, when the earth itself nurtured life. Without that place, there's a sense something's missing, an unsettled feeling. I was lucky. I was stirred by the soft wind in the pines behind our house, the faded Chinese wallpaper, the tarnished silverware that nobody would ever have bothered polishing.

To me the wallpaper was the most romantic thing about the house, and that Cole couldn't see it, couldn't see the romance, made me worry how he would one day meet a girl and fall in love, ever get married. As if I knew anything about romance. Anyway it didn't matter as it turned out, romance is in the eye of the beholder, stays an enduring mystery.

Cole met Ivy, and romance or not, that was it. Everybody told her not to take up with Cole in the first place, but she didn't listen. Ivy marched down the aisle so hard and fast her long white veil caught air behind her. She thought she knew something they didn't. She thought she was the one person on the face of the earth to recognize Cole's potential. But I was his mama and even I thought about giving up on him. Giving him up. A mama can't divorce her child, though. A mama has dreams that bite and hold on like a damn dog.

How they met was during an armed robbery. Cole was robbing the bank Ivy had worked as a teller at for two days total. Cole passed her a hold-up note and flashed the .38 under his wing. Ivy was trying to talk him out of stealing the money as she stuffed bills into a bag because there was just something about him, she said. Something she thought was special. Turns out Cole had written the hold-up note on the back of his parole card, which tells you something right there that maybe special isn't the word for. Ivy caught up to him outside the bank and swapped him the parole card for the money, which tells you something about Ivy that was impressive to Cole. They locked onto each other like radar and neither of them had a chance until the thing fizzled out. Their engagement was smoldering, explosive, Ivy forever stomping to her car and burning rubber down the road to get away from him. She knew what she was in for, but kept hoping. Kept a little candle burning.

Ivy's coming to the prison to say a last goodbye to Cole, though she waved divorce papers at his face and swore she'd washed her hands of him. We're driving to Riverbend together this final time, and we don't even speak a whole lot in the car. Miles and miles. Both our heads are spinning with the thought of what's going to happen, what is there to say? The man we both loved is going to be put to death. Words are small. It's enough she's here, making this journey with me, and I appreciate just the fact of her sitting there. In some ways, none of it feels real. I'm all inside my head, just going through the motions outwardly. Now and then we pull into a truck stop for coffee and so Ivy can use the restroom. I don't mind the coffee out of the machines, but Ivy won't drink it. She wants us to take proper breaks, sit at the counter and drink fresh-brewed coffee, order a slice of pie if we want. Ivy's moved on from Cole, we both know that, and she's clear in stating she's not looking to turn around, retrace her steps back to something not even there, some phantom.

"The past's the past," Ivy says. "It's dead and gone." She can't say it without a tremor in her voice. It's a fight, I know. She pushes her hair behind her ears and looks so young. I feel protective of her. Her skin is pale, lightly freckled, a blush just under the surface. I'm glad she's coming with me, glad of her company even though she won't be a witness to the execution at the end, only the immediate family. Only me. I look at Ivy and see a whole future in front of her. I see her and it makes me look at where I've been, wonder where I'm going next. Only way to be sure where you're going is to plan the trip — and then you have be ready to pack your bags. I've got a lot of bags to pack when the time comes, and it is coming.

Ivy's had an interesting life. She was a child beauty pageant queen. At eleven she was crowned Little Miss Hollywood Babes Superstar. She still sleeps with Preparation H dabbed under her eyes, a trick models use to firm and tighten delicate skin. At twenty-eight, she's a veteran of odd jobs. Ivy's worked in a movie theater, a car wash, a coffee shop, and a used record store. Now she's an artist. She was sitting in her battered Chevy at a traffic light when it came to her what she might really be. She carves faces of presidents into peach pits. JFK, Nixon, Clinton. Apparently people have been carving presidents into coconuts for a long time. Ivy knows a man in Memphis who paints celebrity portraits on grains of rice. At least she doesn't let herself get bored, she's industrious. Ivy keeps asking me what I'm going to do with myself.

"What do you mean?" I ask her.

"All you are is Cole's mother," she says. "You've disappeared, Grace. The real you."

"The real me?" I echo. But I think that's how it is. Being a mother means wiping out all but the faintest trace of who you used to be. It happens. The baby unfurls in the light while you, your wants and fears for yourself, slide back. There in the shadows, waiting in the wings, you haunt your own days remembering life before. Nothing you would trade to change it, just remindful of what it felt like once upon a time to be you. Now and then the person you are still deep down wells up and greets you, a long lost friend. Sometimes, if you listen, you can still hear the sound of your own blood thrumming in your ears, loud as the grass of a summer night. Just that loud and sweet to your ears.

I wouldn't dare tell Ivy about the kind of loneliness I knew. Weeks and months that went by when I could feel my life slipping through my fingers. She'd hate how needy I was. I'd long for a vacuum salesman, a Jehovah's Witness, a neighbor looking for a stray pet, anybody to come knock on my door and sit for a while with me in my living room. Just to make a pitcher of lemonade was welcome. Other times I'd go to the Carpet Emporium and stay for five hours talking to the carpet salesmen. I'd ask them how shag is made, what colors complement blue, what stain-resistant fibers they'd heard about, anything I could think of. I always left before they threw me out.

I used to have friends in the community, people I knew from church I could call on, but as the years went by and police cars parked on the road in front of my house, lights flashing, I let them fall away, or maybe I pushed them away. I kept to myself more and more. I only wished I could have kept Cole to myself too. But he was out on his own and I couldn't keep secret the things he did, even if I wanted to. I couldn't lock him up and hide him away. I couldn't but the state could. They locked him up, let him out, locked him up again, until didn't neither of them know anything else.

I look around the truck stop and I can't get over how normal, ordinary everything seems. Truckers bent over their food and coffee, TV set to the news. It makes me want to shout. This is the last week of my boy's life. Nothing is normal. Nothing will ever be the same. I want to shake them. *Help me.* But there's nothing they can do. If they showed me a simple kindness, I might cry. I cry anyway. I put my head down to hide my tears, hang my head as if I'm praying. I am praying. All I do.

Ivy is in the restroom throwing up. She excuses herself, runs with her hand covering her mouth. She is pregnant with her sister's baby she conceived standing on her head using a turkey-baster. After her sister couldn't get pregnant using more scientific means, she sterilized a $2.95 kitchen baster in the dishwasher, got her husband to make his genetic contribution, then carried it to Ivy. Ivy inseminated herself while standing on her head, leaning against a wall. I think it's generous, a brave gesture on her part to have this baby for her sister and brother-in-law. I hope they appreciate what she's doing. It's not so easy to give a child up. She needs to look ahead to that. She needs to think about sacrifice, the cost. It costs $2.95 to bring a life into the world, $71.50 to end it. Poisons will race through my son's veins to his heart. That's the price he will pay. And me? I want to shout.

SOIL

Soil is the skin of the planet, it covers most of the earth's land surface and can be thick or thin, ranging from less than an inch to many feet in depth. It consists mainly of weathered and eroded rock fragments of clay, sand, and silt enriched with organic matter, the decomposed remains of plants and animals. Soil reclaims and recycles the materials of life using the vast network of roots and fungal threads that run through it. The earth has endless cycles of decay and regeneration. Many cultures have conceived of the earth as the primal womb of life, Mother Earth. From dust to dust, new life springs from destruction.

FOUR

He was gone from me early on. Out acting ugly most of the time, petty crimes and drugs, wrong-headed friends. I guess I don't know what all Cole got up to. He was in and out of custody, different places, young offender detention centers, high- and low-security jails. I never knew where he'd turn up and it got so they wouldn't let me vouch for him anymore. They knew I couldn't control him any better than they could even despite all their rules and lock-ups. He never was easy to keep put. And I never did settle fretting about where he was at. There wasn't hardly a week went by that he wasn't in court, or in jail, or in hospital bent out of shape from fighting. He had a fast trigger.

Each place where he did time had its own code of behavior rules for visits. Some of them weren't so bad and they were pretty similar. One place I remember you could meet outside and they had these picnic tables where you could talk. There were more than a few so-called "picnic table babies" made out there in relative freedom. Sometimes they can't keep their hands off of each other, a man and a woman come only to see him. It's a strong pull, chemical, magnetic, whatever it is, tell it hurts them to feel it. They're restricted to touch but briefly, still

I've seen feet making new art out of love. You see all kinds of things inside the walls, and when you try to look away, you find you can't. I got frisk-searched oftener than not but I would say nobody took my dignity. I didn't once have a strip search or a body cavity search, though I'd heard sometimes they were done to get back at an inmate who'd been causing trouble. They'd come at him through his family. I wouldn't have cared who saw what, as long as I saw my boy after it was done. Shame? That don't ride close.

Cole was in jail on a burglary charge this time and I expected he might get probation since it wasn't all that bad. But he had a checkered history on record they'd be sure to take into account. Cole was still waiting to find out what was going to happen to him. I signed in at checkpoint and went the walk to see him. There were some men in the yard spirited yelling at each other, despite they were toe to toe, and hollering at others in another unit who they knew by voice even if they couldn't see them. Nobody paid me any mind, not so I noticed.

There are no delicate sounds in a concrete prison. Remote-controlled locks clank open and clunk shut, electric gates whir, there are jabbering walkie-talkies, jabbering men. There's no softness. The bed is a steel bunk and next to it is a steel sink-and-toilet combo. The toilet has no seat just a molded steel rim. It's not built for comfort, of course. Comfort would be objected to. Though there are thick walls between the cells, sometimes a man will yammer to himself about his life or motorcycles or basketball, yammer so anybody can hear him droning on in a groove. Cole cut earplugs from the spongy soles of his shower slides and sewed dental floss to them so they wouldn't get stuck in his ear canal. That's how he did. He just went and shut in further. The prisoners get smart about doing for themselves and finding means. That was the first thing I noticed when Cole came into the single visiting room on his side of the glass.

"What did you do?" I said. I didn't mean his crime. There was a voice-activated microphone in the glass to speak through.

He glanced at me sheepish. "What?" He sounded far away through that tiny amplifier, like the ticket-seller at a movie theatre, like there were miles between us.

"Let me see those hands." He was back to being five years old again not wanting to show me something he had hid. His hands were down in his lap but I don't miss much about him. I drink him in, believe me.

Then all sudden he made two tough fists and held them up to the glass. His hands were still cuffed.

H-A-R-D it said, a letter on each of the knuckles of one hand, L-U-C-K it said on the other. "Hard luck," I said out loud.

He nodded.

"Is that what it is?" I said.

"That and some else."

"Those letters look fresh. They hurt?"

"Naw," he said.

"You do them yourself?"

He didn't say anything.

"How'd you get to make a tattoo?"

"Motor from a walkman, bent spoon, ball from a ballpoint pen, guitar string, pelican ink. I'd been thinking about it for a while. Saw some guys do it once."

"Guess I'll be getting you a pair of gloves for Christmas. Guess every Christmas from now on you'll get gloves from me."

He smiled. "You could buy them in bulk. Might be cheaper."

We just sat there then. It wasn't uncomfortable.

"You changed your hair," he said.

"I pinned it up in back."

"There's gray in it."

"You seen that gray before. Just usually I color-wash it out. I should've done that yesterday. You're used to my Ash Blond. I guess I don't look nice."

"You could take the pins out if you wanted to." He took a wait. "I'm growing mine."

"It's long already. You're a handsome boy even in need of a haircut."

"Listen, Mama, you seen Ivy lately?"

"Not too lately."

"I think she's mad at me."

"What else is new?"

"She won't talk to me when I call her. Either the phone rings off the hook and she don't pick up, or I get her and she hears it's me and cuts out. It's driving me crazy. I got to see her. Tell her I'm sorry."

"Sorry for what?"

"I don't know. Nothing. Sorry she's mad at me."

"Son, there's worthier things on your plate. Deeper things you ought to be thinking about. Look at where you are."

He shook his head. "She's it. Front and center."

I didn't say anything. What could I?

"It's like a big tease, Mama. You know? One time, we were in this department store and I threw her down on a showroom bed and we started making out." He paused like he was letting the memory live. "She's a hot woman," he said almost to himself. "Sales dude comes over and asks can he help us? Ivy winks at me. 'What do you think, baby,' she says, 'do we want him to help?' I can't get her out of my mind."

For a glimmer of a second, looking at Cole, I saw him as the man he was, not just my boy grown. Saw him toss his head shake the hair out of his eyes, the stubble of beard. Saw he was a good-looking man, strong, ropey-veined muscles on his arms, his blue eyes lit, thinking about Ivy. Then it was gone. I hoped the color was faded from my cheeks too. I wanted him to feel passionate about Ivy, but it scared me. It made him burn inside.

"Why don't she pick up the phone, Mama? I swear I'm going out of my mind."

The number of times Cole has called me from jail and made his thirty minutes last, ignoring the recording: *You have three minutes left to termination.* He'd carry on talking, be mid-sentence even when there was a click. And nothing. I imagined him holding the phone, only slowly putting it down, rolling himself a cigarette, concentrating on that.

"Maybe she's busy," I said.

He slivered his eyes. "Doing what, Mama? Where the fuck is my wife?"

"You want me to try calling her? I'm sure there's a reason."

"Bet there is."

"Cole, listen to me. You got to wind down and relax. Ivy's taking care of her own business."

He shook his head, agitated.

One thing about Ivy, she knew herself. From the start, she told me she'd given up trying to be perfect. I admired her for that. Fleeting instants of perfection were enough — she'd smile a perfect smile, paint her nails perfectly within the margins of skin — and be satisfied. She wouldn't dream of throwing her life away trying to be so good at everything that somehow she blotted out the mistakes of her man. That was something saved for a fool and a mother. During the roller-coaster of trying to love my son, Ivy mostly managed to keep her confidence intact and treat herself with respect.

"She is where she is," I said. "And you are where you are. When you get back to your cell, why don't you put on the radio, listen to music, something speak easy to you."

Cole cussed under his breath.

Most of the inmates have boom-boxes they listen to with earphones. If they feel like it, they dance in their cells. Nobody else can hear their music but they sing their hearts out to the bare walls. All those men singing off-key, so loud it hurts.

"I got to get out of here," Cole said in a flat voice.

"Well, you will," I said, "in time."

"Sure." He turned his face away. "One way or the other." The color came into his cheeks, and I knew, an electric sizzle into his blood. I'd seen it before, a tight rage.

Then he leaned in closer to me and slow, slow so the guard wouldn't notice, he raised his cuffs and pressed his fingertips to the metal amplifier. He kept pressing and gave it a slight twist clockwise so a narrow space formed between the metal and the glass. Space enough for a razor blade or a cyanide pill. His eyes met mine. A second later he closed the gap and landed his hands back in his lap. He wanted to show me there was an opening, a ready window between this world and the next, an exit he could take. I should have known then he was desperate.

He stood up and that was the end of the visit.

I drove home from the jail, the windows rolled down so the air rushed in my ears and blocked out any thoughts from my head. I went straight to the backyard and got down on my knees and dug. I didn't even have a flower to be planted but I dug a neat hole. The smell of the earth, wet from the night's rain, was musky and rich. An intimate smell. I closed my eyes and breathed. I didn't wear gloves so I could feel the cool soil on my hands. I worked slowly, digging with the trowel, then using my hands to press the earth hard and firm against the sides of the hole. As a child, I dug holes in this same yard thinking I could get to China, come out the other side of the world to the pretty scenes on the living-room wallpaper, the cranberry skies. I used to peer down into the darkness of the earth thinking I would see light, any moment, a ray of light from far away. I scooped soil from the bottom of the hole and heaped it around the outer edges, sat back on my heels, wiped my brow.

When Cole was small I planted a flower garden it gave me pleasure to tend. It contented me to watch the flowers take root and grow. Hours would laze by and I'd keep on digging and planting, peaceful inside myself. The earth was alive with worms and bugs, frogs, the tiniest bustling creatures. I grew four-o'clocks that were their best viewed at night, touch-me-nots whose seeds would explode all over the ground, beds of hydrangea and moss roses, and later old-time flowers and herbs that made healing medicines. I got to know about natural remedies, cures for headaches and the like.

I took the trowel and dug deeper. I liked the way the dark earth filled the lines and cracks of my hands so it seemed they were etched with ink. As though an artist had drawn them. Mama said she could always find me up to my ears in dirt, except for my two green thumbs.

When I was a child I used to travel to Canada in the summers and stay at my aunt's cottage on a lake. Ellen came once or twice but that was all, she rather would stay at home with Mama than risk losing whatever boyfriend she had by being gone. It was as far from home as I ever went and it was when I first really noticed the landscape around me, the color of the soil, how it changed from place to place.

That far north the wilderness is crudely beautiful, with rocky-shored lakes of clear blue water, cold as ice. The oldest rocks in the world are there in the Canadian Shield, four billion years old nearly. Older than stars. Huge tall trees, mixed forests of fir, cedar, birch, oak, maple, and others. Lonely islands with windblown white pines clinging to their rims. In the morning fog those trees were mystical. I was usually the only one standing there looking, and it was a spiritual thing. Afternoons I chased shiny dragonflies like live helicopters, tracked monarchs with bright wings, leopard frogs, grass snakes, woodpeckers, raccoons. Once at night, in the true dark above the horizon, soft green curtains billowed and swirled across the sky, ghostly ribbons moving fast, pulsing and fading. The northern lights.

I loved the hard rocks, fragrant pine needles, sturdy wild-flowers, some that wilted as soon as they were picked, wild raspberries and blackberries. Dark earth on my hands. My uncle had lived in the woods so long he rubbed his back up and down on a tree like a bear scratching while he talked. The cottage furniture was bent willow branches bound together with cord to make armchairs and tables. When she died, less than a year after my uncle, my aunt gave me the cottage in her will. The rental of it to a man who fixed it up so he could live there year round was most of the income I needed to cover my expenses. Mama and her sister both believed in passing down property and I did well by my inheritance from them each.

Kneeling in my garden, I absently reached back to fasten my hair where it had come loose from its clip, a thing I'd done a million times before, but now it brought to mind a summer when I was twelve. Why will a spark flare, and kindle a memory long filed away to burn again? It doesn't seem to matter how many years have passed, how many chapters in the book of your life, it's as if the whole time your mind's been working to connect it all. To prove to you everything had its reason, makes sense in the long run.

There was a couple who lived near to my aunt's cottage on the lake and every day they went out, rain or shine, in their boat. It was a small metal boat painted red with a motor on the back. Out on the water, the wind blew the woman's white hair loose from its clip so it whipped around her face. Sometimes she tried to fasten it back, or else she held her hand on her hair to keep it down as best she could. Sometimes she let it go, let the white cloud of her hair blow around her.

Day after day they circled the lake, drinking coffee from a thermos and sandwiches they brought in a hamper. The man sat in the back steering. If it was cold, the woman wrapped a wool blanket around her shoulders. I felt I knew them because I knew their routine and I'd made them part of mine. I thought it was a hobby for them to motor in circles and they had nothing better to do. I had nothing better to do than watch them.

Some days the lake water was choppy, others it was mirror smooth. I wouldn't have minded being out with them in their boat, not talking much I didn't expect. A great blue heron would lift from a distant island into the air with just a few slow, heavy flaps of its large wings. From the shore I would wave to the couple, and they'd wave back if they saw me. They trawled a net behind their boat.

I found out they were dragging the lake bottom for their sons who'd drowned in an accident. When the boys had drowned — if it was that summer, the summer before, or years before — nobody ever told me. They went around and around searching for the exact spot where something had gone wrong. Hoping to find awful buried treasure beneath the sparkling surface. I wanted them to leave it alone. I was angry, as if they'd let themselves be caught in an undertow, couldn't move on. But had they pointed their boat towards open water and never looked back? If I saw them now, I'd huddle with them against the elements and circle to dredge up the past, scared too of what I'd find.

The phone rang inside the house and I stood pushing my hand against my lower spine, wiping my forehead with my sleeve. Cole had walked out of the jail. He'd stuck a guard with a sharpened metal pipe while he was on work duty on the grounds, and walked out. He was considered dangerous. They gave me a number to call if he contacted me, but I didn't write it down.

I leaned my forehead against the window. There was the empty hole I'd dug. A neat empty grave, just waiting.

TOUCH-ME-NOT

Also called jewelweed. Pale yellow and orange spotted flowers shaped like those of snapdragon but with a spur formed by an extended calyx. The seed pods are explosive capsules that shatter emphatically when touched, shooting seeds several feet. In the early morning, sparkling drops of water often adorn the leaves. Jewelweed in the wild grows near poison ivy or poison oak, and provides a ready cure for the itching rash caused by those plants. A handful of jewelweed may be plunged into water and shaken out, the stems crushed between the palms of both hands until broken up, then rubbed on ailing parts. This treatment relieves skin maladies ranging from rashes to insect bites, to stinging inflammation from nettle, briars, or brambles, deadening the pain.

FIVE

All my life nothing ever went as planned. I met Jackson, Cole's father, late one night in the hospital emergency room. He was getting thirteen shots in his stomach for being bit by a squirrel. He was grinning through the pain, joking with the nurses who were thanking heaven he'd come in on their shift. He had a catchy smile. He teased them all. I was folding towels off in the background when he saw me. I was doing my housekeeping job folding towels, stacking them neat as a pin on a shelf. He winked at me but then he kept looking. I swear when he looked at me like that, he saw me. He didn't look away. It felt like the clouds parted and a sunbeam blazed through, the heat of it. I blushed and I looked away. My heart waltzing in my chest. I looked back at him and he still hadn't wavered, was still looking. He knew he had me.

I liked walking places holding his hand. I liked holding Jackson's hand more than made sense, more than was good. We'd drive around in his truck, drink wine in a place some-where after it got dark, and then he'd take me home. Just being near him was all I wanted. We'd kiss on the porch till Mama flashed the lights. She didn't care that I was old enough and ready for almost anything. She was way too sick to have it in her to worry. She wanted her life, and mine, to be straight on and simple. I didn't need to remind her you can't always get what you want. She knew that all along.

Jackson was a firefighter. He had a wife already and two little kids. He could tell you everything there was about Harry Houdini, the great escape artist. Jackson could tell you about disappearing acts. Harry Houdini could hold his breath under water for three minutes, and took a mean punch in the stomach to prove how strong he was but died a while later, poisoned by a ruptured appendix caused by that blow, or at least made worse by it. Houdini didn't think his body would fail him and he dared it too far, like Jackson. Jackson thought nothing of giving up his oxygen to some poor soul near dead in a fire. Then he'd have to hold his breath, carry the man out on his shoulders. He had to hold his breath if to let both of them make it out alive. He forgot he was only human, the way certain men will turn their backs on the truth about themselves. But you can't escape yourself. There you always are.

Houdini died on Halloween, and every year on the anniversary of his death, his wife held a seance hoping to receive from him the secret message they'd agreed he would try to send from the near beyond as proof of life after death, and more, his everlasting love for her. After ten years Mrs. Houdini held the last seance on top of a skyscraper in Hollywood. Her friend, Dr. Saint, pleaded with Houdini to manifest himself — levitate the table or ring the bell they had waiting. But in vain. Finally Dr. Saint said to Mrs. Houdini that ten years were gone, the zero hour had passed. Had she reached any decision? And Mrs. Houdini answered that she was kissing her last hope goodbye. She did not believe Houdini could come back to her. Good night, Harry, is what she said as she turned out the light on the Houdini Shrine, which had burned for ten long years. If it was that easy.

Jackson and I went swimming summer evenings in a secluded pond with sprawling willow trees on its banks. Jackson had a respect for water matched his respect for fire. He'd take off his clothes and splash into the pond, naked and brown as bark from head to toe, textured like that down his back where fires had crawled up on him. I was slower wading in. I'd unbutton my dress, slip it off and hang it over a branch to keep it clean. My bra and panties were my bathing suit. In the water with Jackson, cool mud beneath my feet, him in my arms, lean muscle under my hands, I couldn't hold myself back. He'd put his mouth on my open mouth and my cries went into him.

Later the water from my underthings bled through my dress leaving wet spots across my chest, hips, and stomach. Jackson would watch me wring out my hair and do my best to untangle it with my fingers. He saw me with mud-caked feet, in a water-mottled dress, and wanted me still. He'd kiss me so hard it hurt. Pull me to him with his hand at the back of my neck. I heard his name in my head, the sound of it, the feel of him. He'd push into me and I would have done anything. When he collapsed onto me, the weight of his shoulder pressing my mouth closed, I traced the lines in his back, dry riverbeds, where the fire had flowed. Above, those big old willow trees bending down over me. They taught me I could weep without tears. I was clinging to a slim thread of hope.

It got to be a dream to spend a night together. Jackson came up with Niagara Falls. He went on about the Falls, the power of the water, the force it had to light up the entire eastern United States with electricity. He saved enough money for us to get on the road and out of town. He came by after a shift at the fire station, picked me up before dawn when everything was still blue and hushed. He slept while I drove the whole way to the Horseshoe Falls. The whole long way. I didn't mind. We'd get a weekend together.

Jackson couldn't ever sleep on duty at the station, not restfully. He was bothered by the sounds of his partners snoring, moaning and groaning having nightmares in their beds, the air conditioning, cars chasing by outside. He'd lay awake smoking, listening to the men in the darkness, a brotherhood like the Marine Corps or like prison. Although I don't think anyone screamed or talked crazy at the fire station, cried out for mercy or forgiveness, revenge, and was ignored by even those who heard. Cole and his daddy both slept among men for most of their grown lives and neither of them ever got used to it.

Jackson kept his bare feet stuck out the side window of the car so they could get the same fine breeze that whipped my hair across my face. That man. Didn't matter to me where I was going, honestly, or how long it took to get there. The radio played and for a single time, a one-shot deal, I got to see Jackson sleep. I put miles between us and his wife. His children we'd left behind like stars twinkling in a breaking sky.

His wife had a French name, Chantel, I couldn't forget. The kids were maybe four and six years old. The boy had glasses that magnified his eyes and made him look big-headed and smart. The girl carted a baby doll by a leg. I saw them hug onto the other, two little forms, until they toppled to the ground rolling like puppies. I used to walk by their house now and then to catch them playing. It didn't seem, not in my mind, that Jackson had a thing to do with them. He didn't tuck them into their beds, read them a fairy story, kiss them goodnight, tell them sweet dreams.

I was invisible, but I made Jackson disappear from his wife and kids too. I blame myself. I messed with the truth and I'm ashamed of it. The truth can be mean, a hard thing to pin down. It can live and take on shapes, change like the weather right in front of you if you don't take care. You can't let yourself look away for a second. And you can't whitewash the dirt gone just because you want to. Even if a man doesn't act like he's married, doesn't mean he hasn't tied a knot.

We got a motel room we drove up and parked the car in front of. Niagara Falls was neon lights and tawdry flashing signs in the daytime, wax museums and fast-food stalls. A seedy, worn-out place full of lie-laced promises. Jackson went to take a shower and I turned channels on the TV. He was still wet, clear droplets of water on his shoulders, when he came from the bathroom with a white towel wrapped around his waist. He came to me, to the edge of the bed like that, and I took it off him. We laid down together as though it wasn't new for us to be on a bed, inside a room instead of on grass or in a truck. We rocked the bedsprings and held fast each other, the headboard banging against the wall.

"Lay back," he whispered. He kissed my throat. "This is for you. Let me do all the work."

Wanting him so much then I could taste it, salt on my tongue, tears and sweat. Such yearning to have him. To have him be mine. "I could love you," I told him. "I would love you so much. I would want you all the time."

"I'm not that great," he said.

He didn't have to believe me — I loved him already. Simple as that, I already did.

"I'm not even worth thinking about," he said.

"Still." I would love him my whole life. If he ever took a step to meet me, I would jump into his arms and never look back.

Jackson was loose wires, restless in a kind of limbo. I could see why he admired an escape artist who could break the chains that bound him with what was either superhuman strength, or superhuman cunning. At the very least, magic. Escape isn't so neat a trick outside the world of illusion.

Jackson was trapped in his life like a bug in a jar. He thought he'd escaped to freedom in Niagara Falls. But he wasn't right. Freedom's not a place you can drive up and park in front of. You make your choices and sometimes, like Harry Houdini himself, everything, even your death, has to do with who you are and how you lived your life. You die the death you made for yourself by the way you lived. In the end, it's crystal clear.

Take Cole. He was lost on the outside. Prison's the only place he ever fitted in. There was nowhere for him. No place he could escape to, had for them to lock him up.

Cole was made then and there in that rickety bed, in the midst of my love, nearby a natural wonder. Maybe I even knew the exact moment we sprung him to life, I think I cried out and it was echoed. Niagara Falls was a force of nature. That's how Cole was. All that hard white water pounding down and down, until it erodes its own foundation to nothing.

Jackson rolled over and I kissed the fire's claw marks on his skin. What it was about fire. Fire was a living, breathing animal Jackson wanted to beat. There were fires his men lost to, buildings collapsed and burned to the ground, people died inside, sleeping or awake, because a fire will fight back. It'll play dead then flare up when nobody's around and finish what it started. It might linger in corners, smolder behind the siding, lick in the rafters of the roof, just waiting.

Jackson was always scared as he should be. A fire can make a house a maze of dead-ends. Once he got lost in a little bungalow, thought he was in hell with no way out. Somewhere swallowed up in the burning house was a toddler and his grandma who was babysitting him. Jackson hoped to find them alive before it was too late, because even if they didn't get burned, they could suffocate in a hurry from breathing smoke.

Jackson and his partners went in with flashlights and air-packs, went in low where the air was cooler, wormed their way forward on the floor holding axes and pike poles to tear down ceilings if they had to. Went in blind. They inched forward keeping one hand on the man in front's shoulder, pulling the hose with them. They could barely hear each other talking behind the masks, their breathing labored through heavy smoke and the zero visibility. The air burned their ears as they sprayed water and crawled towards the heat. Their ears were exposed, delicate flesh sensors, each man's warning device — hot, cold, warm, warmer, burning. Everything was charred and black, the water they were slushing in scorching. Further inside, behind a door, the fire was feeding and getting bigger. A fire needs heat, fuel, and oxygen. The glow of the flames shone on the men's masks. The fire roared as they fought it because it was trapped and they were choking it.

The old woman and the boy were found together on a bed. If luck met them, they slept on until the end and just never woke up. That was a slender mercy Jackson prayed for. I won-der. If the grandma woke and stared at the fire. She couldn't have done a thing by then to protect them but maybe she tried to stare that fire down. She might have locked eyes with it, rag-ing beast, and been helpless. I feel her arm tighten around the boy, pull him close to her.

I know what it is to want to save a child and not be able to. It's worse than harming the child yourself by a thoughtless mis-take: setting him into a tub of scalding water because you didn't check it first, or dragging him along too fast so he falls and skins a knee. Times I have believed Cole ought to have somebody better than me taking care of him. I've understood he deserved at least that. The whole world is a puzzle to me. The way it is. A mother is responsible for keeping her child alive. But how to be responsible for the child's actions, or what he thinks? What's in his heart? Sorry isn't good enough. Take me instead — nobody wants to hear.

I drew letters on Jackson's back, *I love you, I love you, I love you*, that made no impression. Cole knew who his daddy was. He was proud even if from a distance. When he was seven, Cole took a match to the porch and tried to burn down our house so his daddy would come and put out the fire. I won't ever forget the smell of smoke in our hair, on our clothes. The bright orange fire rolling like a river along the eaves of the porch. I was scared that my house would catch, all the things that had been my mama's burn to the ground. I can still feel the heat of the flames on my face, sting of the thick smoke in my eyes and lungs, the wisps of burned newspapers floating up like black butterflies. The dangerous smell of something on fire in the dark.

It was the Fourth of July and earlier that night Cole and I had sat out in a farmer's field, a thin blanket wrapping us both together, watching the fireworks. It wasn't often I could keep him that close to me. If I wanted to I could lean down and rest my chin on top of his head. The stars were so brilliant they competed with the fireworks, they shone that bright in the clear dark. If you closed your eyes, lights still burst behind your lids, dazzling explosions imprinted on your vision. When I looked at Cole, he'd be blushed hues of rosy pink, then he'd gleam soft mystic green, changing as the skies flashed color, washed him in light like a bold aurora.

Jackson was one of the men called on duty that night and he came full speed running the siren, parked the truck at the curb, got the pumper throbbing, hoses primed and ready. Cole stood watching Jackson move amongst the men. They laid the hoses down like snakes in the grass. When Jackson turned his back to take care of the fire, Cole lit a sparkler. He wrote his name in the black air with fiery snowflakes. Over and over his name blazed, faded, and disappeared.

SIX

It was hard to be angry at Cole for setting fire to the porch when I knew why he'd done it. Scared as I was to lose everything, I understood Cole had nothing to lose, in his mind that was why he did it. It was a desperate act. I didn't say too much about it, I knew he was suffering. I tried to stay solid by him, be a rock for him, there when he needed me.

That same summer Cole was seven we watched a solar eclipse together. We saw the light get snuffed out. Used to be people thought eclipses were bad omens, signs of doom from the heavens. They thought plagues would come, natural disasters, wars. I don't think Cole knew what all the fuss was about, clippings from the newspaper I'd save and tack on the fridge. Together we made special cardboard viewing boxes with polarized glass inside, and on the day of the eclipse, we sat in the yard out away from the pines, up on the hill where we had a clear spread of sky, and waited.

Cole was fidgety as usual and I gave him snacks from the picnic basket to keep him occupied — watermelon, crackers, cheese, sodas — till I was worried he might be sick. I told him to listen to the birds, how they'd go to bed when the sky got dark just as if it was night. They'd think it was night. Birds are sensitive. That morning before the tornado when the air was so still and all the birds came out of the trees, laid on the ground. Every kind of bird there ever was, hundreds or thousands of them down on the ground, as though a giant hand had shaken the trees, the birds falling to the earth like figs. Maybe they knew their homes would be uprooted and gone in seconds. If they huddled low, any and all evil would pass over top of them.

You listen, I told Cole, and watch what happens when the sun and the moon play tricks. I explained how the moon was going to get right in line between the earth and the sun, and from where we were, we'd see a total eclipse which happens only once every four hundred years in any given place. Weren't we lucky to be where we were this July day, hot as it was? It's not too often you can say you were in the right place at the right time. I told him ages ago people were scared of eclipses because they thought it meant the sun was being killed. They thought a monster, or wild animal like a dragon, or a lion, or a wolf, had attacked the sun and begun to eat it. Crowds would try to chase the monster off by making a lot of noise, banging things, playing wild music — in protest — to try and save the sun, its golden light. The natural order was upset when the moon stole the sun's rightful place in the sky. People felt uneasy because a law they understood about the way the world works was broken, and that can't happen without backlash. The Gospels tell that on the day Christ was crucified there was a strange, long-lasting eclipse. Nobody cares about omens anymore, but back then they did. Then the weather and cosmic events were signs. Mirrors to see and judge your soul in.

Cole and I sat there peering into the smoked glass in our viewing boxes every other minute to check what the sun was doing. For a long while it just shone like nothing was going on. We were both excited. I was wearing a new dress patterned with ripe berries and sprays of lilacs that clung to me like a silky second skin in the heat. I felt pretty for a change, ready for the world to show me some magic. I guess I'd had Cole back with me a year or so by then and we were used to each other and got along. Cole didn't talk much, he was active and wild. He'd run sooner than walk anywhere, climb and get into everything like I'd always expected a boy to so I wasn't surprised. I had to keep a steady stream of words flowing his way to try to hold him put even then, his legs swung back and forth from the chair, kicking at twigs on the ground with his feet, just always restless at the core. I remember he had a crocodile doll he dragged everywhere with him. I forget what he named it, but he cared for it. Miz somebody. One time he told me the crocodile was his wife. I said, "She's real cute."

"Naw," Cole said. "But she's pointy. She could bite your head off if she took a wanting with her snazzy teeth."

All day long I warned Cole not to look at the sun with his bare eyes since he might be blinded. I knew I was being my own echo, but I wanted him to mind me. I told him, "Hear me. You go looking at the sun, you'll burn holes in your eyeballs and then you won't see anything — neither nice nor ugly — again. Understand?"

I scared him more than I even meant to. After that he wanted to know what blind was. Did it hurt real bad? Was it till you died, or did it go away if you went to sleep? He kept on, chewing it over, asking me this, asking me that. I told him I bet a hot poker rammed in your eye be a better gift. He paled. Then he laughed. A mocking little laugh, bitter on its edges.

He was only seven but Cole didn't like to be bullied. He didn't like to be threatened. I believe he was scared of most things in a peculiar way of his own, and for his own reasons, whatever all they might have been. Scared of the dark, scared of the light, scared of me and himself, the endless things each by each that add up to a day. A laugh like that has worry chasing it. I never did hear him laugh a pure, easy laugh. There was always a tinge of something else — worry, spite, anger — burning its edges. I missed it in a real way, a joyful laugh coming from my child that I could catch and join in.

But it's not true. I did hear him laugh, only one time, a real deep, easy laugh. And I think if you asked Cole, he'd say he was punished for it. Although I never meant it to backfire on him, on us both.

I was always bothered I couldn't make things easier for my son. Bothered we're all shut in tight alone with ourselves, hostage of our own torments. Even a child's mama can't know about his private pains and secret fears, not too much. And she can't trade places to suffer instead. Even if she would, be so willing to take his burdens for herself, carry him on. All she can do is dry her baby's tears on the hem of her dress. Hold him to her bosom if he'll let her, rock him in her arms, if he'll let her.

I never saw Cole peek at the eclipse. I did once despite myself, and when I looked away, a big blue spot glared atop everything worse than the flash from a camera. I didn't need to get struck blind staring at the sun. It was a dumb thing to do, dumb as Lot's wife glancing back for an eyeful. I know it sounds crazy, but sitting there, I got to comparing the sun in the sky with my son. Light. It was summer after all, and my thoughts stretched loose. I could feel the heat on the back of my neck, soaking into my arms and legs. Katydids buzzed in the trees, getting louder as the day grew hotter. I thought just how Cole was the light of my life, gave me a reason why to get up in the morning. I went over and kneeled in the grass in front of him, laid my head on his lap. He had skinny legs in the same denim shorts he wore all that summer and the next one. His eyes were blue as cornflowers when they looked at me, wondering. He let me be there, resting my head. When he smiled briefly, I was uplifted. It wasn't often Cole smiled. He looked serious most times, his narrow lips held in a firm line. Any smile of his took me a long way. I knew to make it last.

"What's the matter with you, Mama?"

"Nothing. I'm just happy."

"Why?"

"Be sitting here with you. Watching the sky."

He looked up. The line of his throat was so pretty to me it almost hurt to admire it. The beauty of this boy I'd made out of the deepest well of my body. I told him, "When that tornado struck, I thought it was the end of the world. All those little girls blown out like candles in the wind. But then you were born and I knew instead I was lucky. You were born out of all that destruction. It wasn't the end of the world, but my beginning."

Cole put his hands over his ears.

"You were the one good thing that came out of all that. Cole?"

He kept his hands cupped over his ears, his eyes closed, shaking his head. He didn't want to hear it. Only later, when he was older, did he tell me how much he hated hearing about the tornado. I never knew before, never thought he felt guilty. I never saw it that way. I just kissed his kneecap, sat back in my chair.

By then shadows were growing on everything as if they were coming to life. The air itself changed and went quiet. Even Cole held still. The light slipped from that glaring July yellow to a thin-washed rose. In the viewing box, the tiny white sun had a dark curve cut out the side of it. I moved our lawn chairs so they were next to each other, almost touching. I winked at Cole because the eclipse had finally started.

The trees hunkered back against the horizon, blurring into each other, objects flattened out making their forms hard to tell. Twilight came down, a dense rich purple. Crickets started to sing in the grass and a lone whippoorwill called from somewhere behind us. Through the hole in the cardboard box, we watched the moon glide on its path to block out more and more of the sun's rays. The sun was just a glittering crescent. The shadows had gone and it was nearly full dark. The temperature dropped by ten degrees and goosebumps pricked my arms where the wind snuck across. Cole was bouncing now on his seat, enthralled by the strange dark.

"Is it night?" he asked me then in a bare whisper.

I met his hush. "The moon is cloaking the sun."

"But what if the sun don't come back?"

"It will."

"What if it don't?" he said.

"It has to."

"Naw, it don't. The sun can do what it wants."

Lightning bugs sparked, stitching dizzy patterns in the moonlight around us. There were stars. More stars than I ever saw before, even on clear winter nights. Stars in the daytime. I pointed out the Big Dipper, Polaris, and the planet Jupiter. So many stars we might have been lost at sea. An owl called from the woods, a dog barked. Hanging in the sky was a big black sun. Spiring around it, a hazy yellow glow from the tongues of flaming gases that licked out millions of miles. For an instant, I wished I'd never brought Cole to see the eclipse. He was staring with his head thrown back, arms flung out, fists clenched at the black sun and its blazing halo, drinking it in. Darkness had taken over the world.

The total eclipse only lasted a minute or two and then the day started to brighten and the birds came back singing like it was a new morning, that sad old whippoorwill. The fireflies kept on their dancing party even after the stars faded. I was chilled. I saw Cole's hair was damped down on his forehead and beads of sweat had broken out above his lip as though he'd caught fever. We folded up our chairs and went inside. I fixed myself some hot tea and trailed close to him after that. He was oddly calm, but his eyes took my breath. They burned. Awful twin suns with the light blacked out.

I set him in the tub, making the bath water into a swamp with rubber snakes, toads, frogs, turtles, alligators, the way he liked it. I scrubbed that child, bathed him like he'd never been bathed, pulling the washrag over his skin, behind his ears, working it inside his ears, until he was some shiny boy. All except for those big black eyes. I dusted him with talcum and sprinkled more on his bedsheets to try keep down the heat in him. That night I slept beside him, waking when he shouted words which had no meaning to me.

The wind came on during the night. The curtains filled like sails and blew, the muggy smell of earth and water. Rain hit the windows like handfuls of thrown sand. My son was restless. He kicked the sheets off us both all night long. By dawn the storm had spent.

I believe it was the eclipse that triggered Cole's passion for the stars. I can still see the summer heavens the way they were that day, cloudless, drenched in afternoon stars, a midnight sun ringed with fire. Nothing the way it ought to be. Cole keeps a map of the night sky taped to the ceiling of his cell. He can name all the constellations, the signs of the zodiac and the others, shimmering with myth. He knows as much about falling stars, comets, asteroids, meteors, as any astronomer. Gazing at the stars was the only time Cole rested tranquil. Something in those pinpricks of light in the blackness caught him up somehow, moved him in place. Whatever else, could be he was grateful to the stars, they let him wander, and be still.

Cole lost his lifetime's only chance to see Halley's Comet when he was in jail. No amount of pleading on his part could get the warden to let him into the yard for even a few brief minutes to look into space. That was hard on him. For Cole, one of the meaner punishments of being locked in prison is he almost never can see the stars. He can see sky, all the sky he wants in the daytime but not ever at night, not ever moonlight. The only time now Cole can hope to see a starry sky is in the winter months if he's taken outside the walls for some reason to court. Then he might be brought back to the prison late enough in the afternoon it's turned early dark. If he looks up then, he might see his stars. They'd be all his.

Those stretches Cole was freed from jail after serving a sentence, or was cut loose on bail, he'd sometimes come hitching home just to sleep in the backyard. Before I went to bed, I'd slip out the screen door and cover him with a blanket. Even if he wasn't asleep, he never seemed to notice my touch. Nothing disturbed him then, not chiggers or mosquitoes or assassin bugs or the raving cicadas and crickets. Those nights under the stars were the most peaceful for him. They were the most free. At sunrise, he'd stroll into the house, cold and wet with dew, and I swear there were stars still shining in his eyes. He had diamonds in his eyes.

FIREFLIES

Even before they hatch they glow in their eggs. Love-lit beetles that flash their sexual morse code at nightfall. Chemicals in their bodies called luciferin and luciferase react with oxygen in their abdomens to create a yellow-green light. Fireflies can produce the light at will, using it to attract mates. Females are able to mimic the flash of other species, flirting to seduce males. Once the males are lit up and draw near, they're eaten. Only 2 percent of fireflies' bioluminescent energy is lost as heat, compared to 97 percent for light bulbs. That is the natural charm of cold light.

SEVEN

Cole was out of jail on the run. In my mind I saw him take up the metal pipe, keep it hid maybe down his pant leg or behind his back, saw him walk towards the guard and the guard go down, his knees giving out under him. I feared Cole was running so far down the wrong road there'd be no way back for him, every turn he took meant another mistake. Gunning it after Ivy. It had all got out of hand, I knew he didn't mean for it to, but he was so driven by temptation that he acted without thinking, smote by her. He was in deep now, maybe for nothing. Nothing but she hung the moon. She hung it and he was where he couldn't see it from behind those bars, couldn't see his wife to keep track of her.

I pulled a chair up to the front living-room window and sat looking out. I guess in the back of my mind I expected he'd come running home to me, sooner or later he would. I didn't hear anything more from the authorities, or on the TV, or the newspaper. My phone didn't ring. It was just me and my thoughts. Cole was running and hiding and nobody knew his whereabouts and I had to pray no news meant good news. He hadn't been caught, he was still free. I sat by the window long as the day practically. He ran and I stayed put, like when you lose somebody and you better stay where you are so they can come find you. Even if what you want is to run after them, you think chasing in circles would be better than waiting doing nothing, but you might miss each other then. Somebody's got to fix a point. Stay there.

Nightfall I'd come away, make a grilled cheese sandwich and a glass of milk in the kitchen, pickled green tomatoes forked straight out of the jar. I always had books to read. Then it was still library books mostly, but I did own some. I'd started a small collection again after Cole ruined my other one. I'd study my herbal healing manuals, take a look at the plant illustrations, pages of native Indian cures for ailments. Sometimes a sickness first took root in the head or the heart as a wayward emotion that turned itself bad, festered then into a body sickness. That seemed right to me. Dire thoughts will sully the system and taint the flux of balance. It was Mama's cancer got me onto healthful concerns.

She was and I was helpless to keep her living and could but stand watch her body war from the inside out. For all the reading I've done, if I wouldn't yet be made stand watch. I miss her finally, it comes down to that. I don't dwell overmuch on the good or the bad of her nature, miss her just as she was.

She had malignant tumors that grew on both her lungs jointly so there wasn't a way to cut them out and leave her whole enough to survive. I looked after her at home, a death sentence looming over us nigh on six months. She coughed and spit up blood most of those months. Nothing anybody could do, doctors either. No matter where I was in the house, I'd hear her cough and a wave of panic broke over me, my mama coughing and not getting any better. That was the first time in my life I faced a sickness that wouldn't quit and be gone of its own. There was no medicine for it.

Two weeks before the end, she wouldn't eat or drink, just wanted to sleep in her darkened room. The way an animal does, tuck down and die. I tried giving her strawberry milk-shakes with an egg stirred in she could sip through a straw. It hurt her to swallow, but more than that, she didn't want to eat. There was a smell now to her, awful blood smell that came from the rattle in her chest and out her open mouth when she breathed. I tried just about everything to nourish her, she only looked at me like she was sorry for me, laid down in her bed with her eyes closed so I'd leave her alone.

I didn't leave her alone. I couldn't. I sat on the edge of her bed watching her closed eyelids, pale and fluttery wings, the dried skin of her lips. Maybe she knew I wouldn't leave. If sheer love could move mountains couldn't it keep her like this, no worse, this sick but on and on? I climbed under the bedcovers with her and pressed myself to her soft flannel back. The new life my belly held had jutted already, I felt it between us. I was going to be a mother. Would one day my child come in bed with me as I lay dying? If only. Mama needed to go to the hospital at the last where morphine eased her fade. The way it was explained to me, she died by drowning. Her own blood filled her lungs.

Late into the night I'd put my books down, curl in a big armchair and watch TV until I couldn't keep my eyes open. I wondered if a news bulletin would flash about Cole. Where he was? Was he with Ivy, found a haven in her arms, or had the arm of the law got him? Here I was in my living room, one wall stained by honey from bees that sometimes built their hives behind the plaster. The curtains sucked in and out at the windows. A clock on the mantel told the time, there was a vase of flowers from the garden, a candle with fern leaves pressed into the wax. I had no plans to change anything. Even up north at my aunt's cottage my childhood summers, I'd watch the Canada geese take to the sky migrating south for the winter, wonder where did they think they were going? If they stayed, they'd get used to the climate, they'd adapt. Eventually it would be all right. But they'd fly off at the weather's whim, honking in their magnificent V-formation until it was just me left there. Pretty soon I had to follow them south, but I never wanted to leave. I never liked fleeing because the temperature ran hot or cold.

Daylight hours I sat in vigil at the front window. Outside a black dog was skulking around, chewing grass. It had a bad limp when it walked, seemed to tender a front paw. I watched it for some time to see if it had a place to go or somebody would come fetch it. After a long while nobody did so I went out. It was sprawled on the dirt shoulder of the road, panting in the heat.

"Hey boy," I said, crouching down to him, chucking under his chin. "What's up with you, huh? You a stray dog? Where's your collar?"

I lifted the sore paw and it was a mess, cut and a spike of glass wedged deep. I patted his head, poor thing. Told him, "You better come on with me, clean you up. Come on." The black dog got to his legs and I encouraged him follow me home. "Let's go, fella," I said.

We went slow. I was thinking what to do for him. In the backyard I put some water into a bucket and washed off the paw so I could see better the injury. He growled a low rumble, didn't like me touching him where he was hurt. I pulled the glass shard out of a piece, it wasn't so deep as I'd thought at first. The dog gave a yelp, acted like he might want to bite me, baring his teeth, but that was all. I went to the fence and tugged up some plantain, an ugly weed makes a good salve for healing body sores. I laid some of the leaves on the cut and wrapped others around his paw, taped it firm with bandage. Then I brought him out some cold cuts from the fridge. He ate them, licked his lips, and I gave him more.

When I went into the house the black dog trailed in behind me. He wouldn't let me out of his sight, tailing me like a shadow. I told him, "Take it easy. I'm not sorry you're here."

I was just small when my daddy worked nights caretaking at a vet's office and animal shelter. He had to mop the floors and such, clean out the cages. When he took me with him, I skipped straight to the dogs, mostly strays, some puppies. All kinds of dogs there in cages. I'd kneel down, poke my finger through the bars to scratch their noses. They could make some noise barking and whimpering. I felt so sorry for them, way they'd scramble over each other to get my affection, look so winningly at me. I tried to pat each one. I couldn't help myself, one time I went and unlocked all the doors, let them out. Even a sick dog or two came out of his cage and scooted wild, clamoring, frisky amongst the others. I remember how lush it felt opening those doors and loosing the dogs, setting them free. I was twirling around, giddy with it, when I heard my daddy coming down the hall in his boots. He threw me across the room but it was worth it.

The black dog kept keen by my side. A thunderstorm blew in that night and he didn't like it. The wind picked up the leaves in the trees set them sizzling like bacon in a pan. Every complaint of thunder seemed to get under his skin. He tried but couldn't settle, paced back and forth, circling with his ears cocked, sniffing the air. The curtains were full gauzy phantoms he kept wide away from. Cracks of lightning stopped him in his tracks. It was humid so the back screen door was open to the barely cooling breeze. Nothing to see when you looked out the door but sheet darkness. Still the black dog went and pressed his nose to the screen, peered out like he could see something in the near beyond that I couldn't.

I stood behind him shielding my eyes as though it was bright, when it was the polar opposite. I could have been blind. Then there was a sudden vivid flash of lightning and the trees on the edge of the woods lit up so you could see them. The dog barked. He didn't let up. "Hush now," I scolded him. Another sharp flash and the sound of a crackle nearby. In the brief instant of illumination, I thought I saw the figure of a man standing next to a tree. The dog barked, straining louder. We waited walled in by blackness. Then the trees instantly visible, bone-white light, and the figure gone. "Oh, hush. We're just spooking ourselves." I pulled him back away from the door and shut it.

I tossed in bed picturing Cole a fugitive. He had always wandered. He wandered and he erred. My pleading couldn't keep him home any more than a tide pulled from its shore by a beckoning moon, or a wolf to roam. Chasing down the wrong kind of paradise. Whiskey and women, then only Ivy. Paradise to him, chasing what he wanted without thinking what he was doing or where he was going. I pictured him wading up streams, running, hiding, being hunted. Heard the shouts of men and canines in the fast-closing distance. Saw a car crawling lightless along the highway. My son hurtling forward through the woods, staggering blind, branches clawed fingers grabbing at him. Shouts nearer. Halt! My boy falling, lurching up, running on. Then a shot and he crashes to the ground. A bullet in his back. I fall to my knees, turn him over cradling his head. His eyes stare up at me, his mouth open, teeth like dirty rubies. I breathe worlds of air into his chest, lost worlds. In my sleep, I moaned, woke myself up.

I found a note the next morning, slipped under the door from Cole. It must have been him there on the fringe of the woods lit by lightning. I should have known the shape of my own boy. He'd been scared off by the barking dog. But he had come home. The letter said, *Lock up the dog. Put a vase on the windowsill when it's clear to get with you. Cops might be watching the house, hard to tell.*

My heart was pounding. I took the dog to the cellar and fixed him a rug bed on the floor. Then I got the vase of flowers from the mantel and set it on the sill. I let my eyes search out the window to the back of the yard and the clutch of trees beyond where I'd seen Cole in the dark rain. All those days I sat with my chair pulled up to the living-room window looking out, looking for Cole, and now he was near, maybe looking in. I fussed with the flowers, petals fell from the roses as I pushed them around. I felt eyes on me, my hands were shaking.

Time passed, where was he? Why didn't he come? I baked a honey-glazed chicken and an angel cake. I was skittery, jumping at the slightest sound. Hours went by. I checked the vase, moved it more to the center of the sill. I held a rose petal between my fingers, soft as a kiss, the feel of Cole's skin when he was a baby and I'd breathe the sweet scent of him. I looped around myself, restless, like the black dog when the wind came on.

Then he was. He was there in front of me, my son. I let out a cry.

"It's okay," he said.

He looked dirty and he had shadows under his eyes but he gave me one of his rare smiles. He was looking at my empty chair by the window, he knew what it meant. I could see it pained him. "Mama," he sighed, "you can't wait for me."

I went and put my arms around him and I wouldn't have let

go. I'd wait for him always, wait for this, him in my arms. I wouldn't have let go if he didn't pull free of me.

"I can't stay, Mama." He was dodging the window, keeping hid. "I want you to meet me tonight. Alright? I got to be fast out of here. Don't cry. Meet me in the woods by that stump? You know the one. Okay Mama, be there? I got to go. I'll see you tonight after midnight."

"Wait." I had a million words jumbled on the tip of my tongue and I couldn't get but one out to be said. Even that was fair choked. "Son," I said.

"I got to go, Mama."

I pulled him to me again and held him crushed. The hard muscles of his shoulders quivered with the strain of him gripping me back. Everything in the world dropped away. Even the ground seemed to fall away because he had to steady me on my feet when we released.

I straightened myself up. "I made you a meal," I said. "Take it with you." I hurried to the kitchen and put the chicken, some buttermilk biscuits, the angel cake in a sack.

Cole opened the fridge.

"What do you need?" I asked.

"Something to drink. Beer?" he said.

"There's none." Then I remembered an old bottle of George Dickel up in the cupboard, how long it had been there, had dust on it. I took it down.

"Tennessee whiskey," Cole said. "That's a fine meal, Mama."

He took the sack, kissed my cheek in one motion. Then he was gone, vanished same as in the storm. A figment of my wishing eyes, more ghost than man.

POLE STAR

Polaris, the Pole Star, is not the heavens' brightest star but it is the most important because of its fixed location. Mariners used it to navigate stormy seas since it is the only star that keeps its place in the sky. The rotating Earth makes it seem as if the whirling procession of stars circles Polaris while it remains immobile. To ease hard-straining muscles, many species of birds migrate at night, when the air is less turbulent and cooler. Radar has detected waves of up to two million migrating songbirds on clear nights. Heavy rain or cloud grounds them. Night migrants follow the stars, orienting themselves towards the Pole Star for direction.

EIGHT

Justice wears a blindfold. I think of her, froze in stone, nights I roll the years back and see Cole, always a troubled child. My goal was to make us a family, him and me. I wanted him to come up feeling secure. Sending him off to live with my sister's family from the age of two till he hit five was a mistake. That was a big mistake I made, I admit it now. If I could do it again I would do it different. There's a lot of things I would change. Then I guess I had ideas what a real family should be, and on my own, I wasn't it.

I missed seeing my son develop and his character take shape without me. On the surface they did their best, Ellen and Ronny. Just like on the surface they looked the perfect family. Cole didn't get spoiled but when he got up in the morning he had the basics, clean clothes to wear and food on the table. He'd play outside, then at lunch, my sister would call the boys in and there'd be homemade soup and a glass of milk waiting. I hope she had a kind word for him, that she kissed him goodnight.

A normal routine was what mattered I thought. And I believe it does. But where was I? It wasn't normal for Cole to be sharing somebody else's family, tagging along in their life. I know it was how he felt because he's since told me. He thought

I didn't want him. Love him either. The heartache that has caused me. I thought they could do for him more than I could. What little kid wouldn't trade a new pair of shoes for his real own mama? But what mother would have her child go barefoot when it seemed there was a better way? Ellen was more capable than I was. I thought so then, had for most all my life. Even given all the thinking I did, weighing it one way and the other, still my thinking was flawed. I tried to read Cole but I read wrong. I should have known better.

Every day to me then was a day gone. To bring light and sound, faces and bodies into my room, I kept the television set on if I was home. I worked nights mostly and went to bed when the sky broke, paled. I cooked myself meals that weren't balanced and washed my clothes and cleaned the house. I went for walks. Sorrow was by my side. To have borne a child and given him up, I had no peace. There was nobody could fill the gap he'd left. Jackson about that time moved away near Piedmont. He was gone for two years before he came back again. I couldn't think of a single person save Cole I wanted to be with, least of all myself. I was one-minded about it. I missed him like a hunger. I knew the next day would take the same strength and rituals of this one, and I didn't know how long I could march, keeping misery at bay. I missed my son. There is no way to tell how much.

I never thought, believe it or don't, I was being selfish. I guess I thought it was brave of me to sacrifice my time with Cole so instead he could be happy. I thought I was giving him happiness, doing what was best for him. I was giving him a mother, father, and brothers like on television shows, or the all-American Dream. There they were in a neat package, the right ingredients like a TV dinner. But the truth about sacrificing my son — the word cuts twice. To me it meant surrendering my boy, for his sake alone, so he could claim more than I could give him. I put his betterment first, above and beyond my own hurt. I really believed that. But I sacrificed my son. Meaning I offered him up to be destroyed. I gave him up both ways.

This is why — if it seems small, understand it didn't feel it — the earth jolted under my feet. It was at Ellen's, the one and only time I heard Cole laugh a pure deep laugh, he was horsing around with her boys in the yard. He looked the happiest I'd ever seen him. And it was just that, added on top of Ellen's pointing out all the mistakes mothering I made, swayed me to give him up. That child's joyful laugh. So many times after it echoed in my mind, always buoying me up and giving me new strength if ever I doubted my judgment, I'd done the right thing. Now to think I regret my son's one true laugh. But I don't. I only wish I never heard it.

I saw him to visit. I always waited to hear that laugh again, every time. Cole was like a magnet to me, I couldn't keep from touching him somehow, had to put my hands on him and pat his head or squeeze his arm, crazy for him. Maybe it was to make him real to me, the way you pinch yourself to prove you're not dreaming. I admired all his gestures, whether it be tugging up his pants, or rubbing his eyes with his knuckles when he was tired. I took him presents at Christmas and on his birthdays. I didn't know what toys he had already, and sometimes I could tell he was disappointed with what I brought, after he'd opened the spangled wrapping and a GI Joe or Lego landed in his lap identical to those he owned already, and was sick of playing with.

"Thanks," he'd say, turning the thing between his hands, like he was turning it over in his mind too, wondering why did she get me that?

"Do you like it?"

He'd nod. But then he'd put the thing down on the floor and wouldn't pick it up again.

I got him a corduroy shirt in a color to match his eyes, but children don't care for clothing as a gift generally, boys don't.

Ellen said, "You should have checked with me before you went shopping. I could have told you what to get."

She knew and I didn't. It wasn't her intention to be mean, but if she'd slapped my face it would have hurt less. Being reminded my son wasn't mine to have and hold, she knew him better than I did, I had to swallow my pride, it stung worse than a swarm of bees. I told myself this is what I chose. I scolded myself, Ellen knew better. I wouldn't wish that low feeling back, not on anybody.

Cole's birthday came at Easter and one year, I think the year he was four, I thought I'd surprise him. He'd gone to sleep, he had his own bedroom at my sister's, and she and I had sat talking in the den long after midnight. Before I left I told her I wanted to kiss him goodbye. She didn't want me to because it might wake him.

"I'll be quiet," I said.

"He's a light sleeper, Grace."

"I won't make a sound, I promise. Please."

She let me go, couldn't have not let me. I crept into Cole's room barely breathing. He had a gentle face when he slept, no frown or lines of worry. When he was deeply asleep, as he rarely was, he was still.

In my bag were a dozen chocolate bunnies I'd made myself from scratch using a candy mold. I took them out and placed them all around his head on his pillow. He looked so cute, like an Easter dream. I wanted them to be the first things he saw when he woke up in the morning. Where'd all these little bunnies come from? he'd wonder. He might eat them right away for breakfast as a treat. I thought it'd be a sweet surprise for him.

But then. Cole tussled in his sheets, and by morning, the chocolate had melted over everything. It was in his hair, on his face, hands, the bedding. He didn't know what the hell it was. Ellen said she had a hard time calming him down. He screamed his head off so she almost had to call the doctor to come and ease his fit.

"I don't know what you were thinking," she said. "Next time you want to surprise somebody, would you mind asking me first so it doesn't backfire in a bad mess? Can you manage that?"

"Don't worry, there won't be a next time. Tell him from me, I'm sorry. Apologize for me I should have thought better."

I went and got him back when he was five and I'd gleaned the world was imperfect. We were a family, Cole and I, we just were. Most everything that's been around has nicks and flaws, hard times leave their mark. You have to know to respect the dents. There was no such thing as a perfect family, perfect anything. Something I still have to keep reminding myself.

I went and took him back when I saw a thing I'd never seen before, though it must have been right there in front of me if I'd just opened my eyes. So many events in my life, landmark moments, I never saw coming. I was somebody didn't look too far ahead, and for a long time, I didn't look behind me either. I had all I could handle in the present. But I got blindsided, hit hard, only myself to blame. After I went to visit him, Cole never said goodbye to me when I was leaving. He always disappeared before I left, it just seemed he did. Ellen used to make her guests shuck their shoes at the door when they came in her house, so I'd be there collecting my purse and putting my shoes back on in the entranceway when Cole would make himself scarce. It was usual I'd call out goodbye and he wouldn't answer. I never got a goodbye from him. But I didn't give it a second thought.

I always figured he was off playing with Ellen's boys, maybe laughing that laugh just outside of my earshot. He was too busy having fun to notice I was going. Then it was after his fifth birthday, I was backing out of the drive, and I saw him up in his bedroom window. I only happened to look up and there he was, watching me from behind the curtain. Watching me leave. I saw his little face in the window, little pale moon behind the glass. My foot touched the brakes.

I should have gotten out of the car right then, gone up the stairs and gathered him in my arms, carried him away with me. But I waved. It was only when I was lying in bed that night thinking about him, replaying the things he'd said and done, it sank in. He couldn't stand a goodbye. He wanted me the way I wanted him. I felt it like a horror. I hadn't done what was best for my son, giving him up to Ellen, taking him from his real mama. I had made him suffer. I broke out in a sweat and I shivered at the same time, chilled through, suddenly gone feverish. Tears were too good for me, I didn't deserve to let myself cry. I got out of bed and dressed in my clothes.

I went into Cole's old room from when he was a baby and I'd brought him home from the hospital wearing that little knitted bonnet, blue as a robin's egg. I pushed the furniture around, flung open the window, made up the iron daybed with fresh sheets. There was still an old teddy bear of mine on the dresser and I found a ribbon in the drawer and tied it around his neck in a bow. The bear had button eyes, brown and shiny, and I thought he had sympathy for me and I felt my chin tremble holding onto him, wanting to cry. I set him down on the pillow on the daybed, my hands shaking. The room looked bare but I could imagine Cole sprawled on the floor, coloring pictures with crayons we'd tack on the walls later as art. It'd be his place, he'd make it his own.

In the kitchen I brewed a pot of coffee and baked some oat-meal cookies, stacked them on a plate on the table. I kept see-ing Cole's face behind the curtain at my sister's, watching me leave, saw myself waving and driving off. I was haunted by it. I checked the clock, slow circling of the second hand, looked at my reflection in the dark kitchen window. At first light I drove to Ellen's.

She didn't want him to come with me. Ellen pulled her bathrobe tighter and cried it was spiteful, mean to take him from his familiar setting, rob him of his kin.

I nodded, still I told her straight. "I'm grateful to you, but he's mine. I'm his family."

Which made her laugh. My sister cut her eyes at me. "What are you going to do when he gets sick, huh? What are you going to do if he wants to join the boy scouts?" On and on, what was I going to do?

"I don't know," I kept saying.

Cole just stood there with his arms at his sides, looking at the ground. One point, she grabbed hold of him and he still just stood. Ellen bent down to his level and asked him outright, did he want to stay with her and the boys in his nice room, or go live with me?

"It's up to you, angel pie," she said, putting her hand under his chin to raise his head so he'd look at her, but still he kept his eyes cast down. "You know you can stay with us as long as you want, that'd be fine with us. Or try make it out with your mama." She was working to smile through her tears, her mouth quivering.

Cole shrugged and I said, "He's coming with me."

I took his hand and fairly pulled him to the car. His legs were wooden but I got him shoved onto the seat, locked the door and closed it. He didn't try to budge. That was a big deal to me. He didn't resist, no kicking or screaming.

"What about his things?" Ellen called in a wavery, lovelorn voice.

I looked in through the window at my son. He was just sitting there, caught maybe he felt, or rescued. A dose of both. I know he looked puny and vulnerable to me, his head hung low, hands in his lap. But he wasn't too small to fill the empty space inside me. I had a hollow that grew so to fit him as my womb once had. The emptiness I felt without him was no more and no less his size. I tapped on the window glass, and when he glanced sidelong at me, I blew him a kiss. He didn't flinch or grin either. It just was what it was, I guess, to him.

"Grace?" Ellen called. My sister was wringing her hands.

"I'll come fetch his stuff later," I told her. But I never did. Cole was all I needed, and whatever he needed, I'd get it for him somehow. I left her standing there in the yard, I couldn't get away fast enough, tires spinning up clouds of dust. It wasn't fair to her. I never thanked her, just came and snatched back my boy. We drove off at breakneck speed, the sun in our eyes, and when Cole turned to look back, all he could see was the clouds we were in. They might have been made of sand and grit off the road, but we were flying.

Cole and I made up our own rules as we went along. At our house he was let to jump on the couch, and if you walked by, he'd spring on you sometimes. He took apart his bike and the toaster and the radio. He couldn't always put them together again, but I think he figured out how they worked. We fought, I won't say we didn't. We raised our voices. I wasn't used to a child. I threatened and bribed him to make him do what I wanted. I threatened to take prized toys away, made him promises of extras — he could stay up an extra hour at bed-time — all to try hopefully just to get on. I didn't find him easy to control. He was forceful about doing what he wanted.

I can tell you we said things to each other that maybe we thought in the heat of the moment were shooting blanks from a gun, but if you got hit, it hurt you. You felt the burn. You don't want to aim a gun at somebody you don't mean to wound. Go into a place waving a toy pistol around and for all anybody knows it's the real thing. Don't they take you down with a real bullet just in case? To be safe, to protect themselves, won't they draw and fire on you?

One of the things Cole and I liked doing was seeing movies at the drive-in. We'd buy a bucket of popcorn, put it on the seat between us, and watch whatever happened to be playing. We didn't care if the movie was an action thriller or a romantic comedy. Cole was still small enough he mostly played in the car, fogging up the windows with his breath and drawing pictures with his finger, usually a crooked little house, or a stick man with two big eyes and circles for hands, as if they were balled in fists. Now and then he'd glance at the movie screen, he liked car crashes. He almost always fell asleep in the middle of the show and I watched the end alone, his head in my lap. He thought it was fun to wear his pajamas in the car but after it made it easy, carrying him into the house, sliding him into bed.

One time Cole had fallen asleep and I was so thirsty I decided to sneak and get a coke from the snack bar. I made sure to shut the door quiet so I wouldn't wake him up, figured I'd be gone all of five minutes going and coming back. I was stand-ing at the counter ordering when I saw him out the window running between the rows of cars. I could just see the top of him, shoulders of his pajamas, tousled hair, but I saw the panic on his face. I ran after him, chased calling his name. He didn't slow, weaving in and out of cars, frantic. I kept calling his name. I kept calling, "I'm here. I'm here."

When he finally stopped and turned, his chest was heaving, his face wet with tears and sweat.

"Baby," I said. "I wouldn't leave you, I was just getting a drink." I put my hands on his cheeks to kiss him but he threw them off, stepped back away from me. His hands were clenched, his eyes so angry, narrowed and glaring at me.

"I wasn't gone but a minute or two," I said. "I'm sorry I scared you."

He crossed his arms in front of his chest. "I wasn't scared," he said.

"You weren't?"

"Naw. I don't care if you go."

I thought of him at Ellen's, saw his face again in the window watching me leave all those times. He must have stood there behind the curtain, by himself, not knowing what to do. He couldn't do anything but get left behind.

"Well, like it or not, I'm not going anywhere, guess you're stuck with me," I said.

I tried to hug him, even with his arms folded, a rigid barrier between us, but he twisted away. Going back to the car, he made it so I had to walk ahead of him while he trawled along behind me. I knew I owed him something I wasn't sure I could ever pay back. Trust in my love. I'd have to prove it to him. We walked down the rows of cars, some with couples necking in them, others packed full of kids, a rippling sea of cars. Cole and I adrift, floating, only him and me. But we were keeping our heads above water.

We got it worked out after a while so it ran pretty smooth. Cole liked to do things his way and I tried to give him the space he needed when he wanted it. He didn't make friends easy, didn't take to the notion of sharing. Sometimes a boy would come over and Cole would give him one of his cars to play with from a convoy of vehicles he had, and just when the kid was having some fun speeding it in the dirt, Cole would snatch it off him. I'd hear their voices floating in through the window, high and jumpy as cats on hot tin.

I'd take them out a tray of biscuits to lift their mood but it wasn't long before Cole was left playing by himself. More than once he loaded chinaberries into a slingshot and chased his friend off like that. I'd be inside, shafts of sunlight filtering through the lace curtains stenciling a pattern on the floor peaceful and still, I'd hear him and look out. There Cole would be, crouched over smashing the car he'd wanted so bad with a rock. The car he'd snatched back only to wreck. I'd knock on the window glass and he'd see me, his hand hovering with the rock in midair before he'd flip it aside. He knew I didn't take to destruction and right back then he still cared to mind my view.

Cole would jump on his bike and tear around the yard then, pedaling wild, fast as he could standing up in the seat. He'd chase around and around, the bike wobbling crazily under him, tires digging a deep rut in the dirt. As if he was trying to bite his own tail, whirling like a tornado caught up in its own fury, whirling until he was spent.

At night I laid down beside him on his bed because he was scared to fall asleep on his own. He'd fight closing his eyes, even tired as he was, his breathing quick and shallow from fear. I'd whisper the Twenty-third Psalm.

"The Lord is my shepherd, I shall not want. He maketh me to lie down in green pastures. He leadeth me beside the still waters."

I'd stroke Cole's back in overlapping circles until I felt him calm. If I stopped too soon, he'd wake and cry out, as if my hand served a medicinal purpose.

"Leave the light on, Mama," he'd say.

"The dark's a blanket, close your eyes, it'll tuck you in."

"You got to leave the light on, Mama, can get smothered in a blanket."

I wanted him to know always he could call me, call *Mama*, in the depths of the night and I would tend to him, drape a soothing voice over him. No matter how old he got he wouldn't need to be alone in the dark.

"Surely goodness and mercy shall follow me all the days of my life."

I meant to comfort him. *Surely goodness and mercy shall follow me all the days of my life.* But I hear that line, such an arrogant plea, and it chills me. No kindness ought ever be taken for granted, nor mercy ever expected. Not when God will strike down pretty children under His own roof.

You can't expect a slow backwash of love to come from your child, which maybe I did expect, or at least I hoped for. Even if it was somewhere far back in my mind, I hoped Cole wouldn't stay mad at me for mistakes I made. I know if anger takes root inside a body it'll grow a bitter weed, choke out anything, everything else. But even being his mama didn't give me the power to look inside him and see what was there. I had to watch him from the outside like anybody else, watch what he did.

Cole helped with the household chores, yard work, and repairs. He tried to act the man of the family earning money for himself with a paper route. He was eleven by then. Sometimes I'd drive him if the weather was grim, and it was a special prize those empty roads in the pre-dawn dark, singing to the radio, just us. Superior we thought to the sleeping many because the time, the night, was ours. It belonged to us. Only our voices singing those old songs. That charmed feeling can't be bought, not with silver or gold.

We weren't bad off, others have less, but compared to Ellen and hers we lived lean. Compared to her kids, Cole had nothing. Could be he thought about that more and more and wanted what they had. Of all the pieces went into his design, one connected to the other as bone to bone of his frame, there was that. He wanted to get some what he didn't have. Wanted it so in his mind it tasted like sugar to him. He must have looked at his cousins and shaken his head, wondering why the cards fell where they did. I just had to mention Ellen's name and he turned stony. He begrudged her, maybe the house she had, the family. He was still child enough to miss having a father to model after. Hard to grow into a man if you never had a real example. There was that especially.

Jackson came by nights when he'd been drinking, found me at the bottom of his glass. He suffered bouts of depression hit him unsuspecting low blows. He'd wend his way over to where I was, an urge to lay with me carrying him on. He'd come to the back door and knock if it wasn't too late, or either throw stones at my bedroom window if it was. I'd look out and see him standing there with a six-pack.

Cole knew who he was and Jackson knew Cole was his boy. The odd occasion they were in a room together, they gulped eyefuls of the other when they thought nobody saw. Neither of them wanted to start anything up and talk. Not that they were shy, but they held at arm's length, as if they knew it couldn't go anywhere, day to day nothing would change.

Those nights were about thirst. Most times they didn't meet anyway because Cole was long in bed sleeping and Jackson fled soon after he came. I never did turn him away and I wasn't ever unhappy to see him, that's just how it always was with me. I had a thirst of my own to quench and I drank until I lost being parched. Jackson would cup my breasts and suckle like my baby never had. He got from my breasts what he needed and I let down and gave to him. I would have given him anything he asked. It was enough for me. If I longed for more, I'd got used to living without it. It was better than nothing. A drop of water is something when you're in the desert. But for Cole? It wasn't enough. Not nearly. A taste only made him more thirsty, know what he was missing.

The other place Cole saw Jackson was at the site of a wreck. The emergency lights flashing red and blue lured a crowd who wanted to witness a tragedy. Cole'd race his bike to get there, stand around with a group of kids looking at the fire trucks and ambulances strung in a line down the road, engines left running. Same model trucks the boys used to play with, speeding them in the dirt, their voices mocking frantic sirens.

One time a car had crumpled into a big oak. The front end was a nightmare of twisted metal and broken glass. The old man driving had suffered a fatal heart attack at the wheel. By the time the rescue crews arrived, a four-year-old girl was in shock in the backseat. She couldn't tell them her name. She didn't know how old she was, or where she came from. Somebody put a blanket around her and lifted her out of there.

Cole watched from the shadow of Jackson's fire truck. When his father came near, he stepped into the light. Jackson's gait faltered, he hesitated. Cole threw himself forward and grabbed hold of him, hugging him tight around the waist. That was something I never thought I'd see, could hardly through my tears. It was a picture to me, a dream glimpse of a life that could have been. It seemed to last and last, even after Cole loosed his grip, Jackson stayed with his arms resting on his boy's shoulders. He stood off from his son, looking at him, letting some current pass between them. Electricity fused them together. Then Jackson dropped his arms stiffly, climbed into his truck and drove off.

Cole scanned the crowd seeming dazed by the tangle of activity. See him then and his eyes were blank, ask him anything and there was no answer to it. I just had to go and pick up his bike, put it in the trunk of the car, take him from the spectacle. He looked out the side window watching everything pass.

Accidents are random as love, no way to prepare or trick yourself into safe readiness. Jackson flipped his car into a ditch after spending most of the night drinking in his barn. When they found him, his golden retriever Prince was chasing circles around the wreck. The car was speeding when it flipped and rolled to rest upside down on Jackson, pinning him inside between the roof and the ground. A crew came from the fire station, some were his partners, to free his legs using the Jaws of Life. I bet he joked with them the while as they worked to loose him. Or maybe not. Maybe it happened another way. He held one of their hands crushed in his, held it though his palm was slick, damp from pain and fear, begged, "Don't leave me, friend."

Jackson recovered from the crash but he had to learn to walk again, slide-shuffle one foot in front of the other. And he couldn't be a firefighter anymore. He couldn't face too many people, friends he'd had. He didn't want to be but a hermit keeping to solitude, and hardly doing a thing except drink for real. Wasn't nobody could talk to change his mind. That went on two years. He wasn't recovered as everybody'd thought.

It was his girl found him. His daughter came home from school to find Prince whining at the garage door. The dog was jumping and barking at her feet, and she didn't know what was wrong with him. The girl hoisted the garage door up and got a rush of bad air. The dog whined and wouldn't go in. A hose ran from the tailpipe to the interior of the idling station wagon. Jackson was dead on the front seat, his cheeks pink, blooming roses the girl thought, from the carbon monoxide.

Cole knew before I did. Everybody was talking about it, there was a long obituary in the local newspaper. It affected Cole deeper than I ever would have thought, given how Jackson wasn't a major figure in his life. I never got to live with Jackson but he was mine in my dreams, gone with the light when I woke. And he wasn't in Cole's life but he somehow was in his heart, same as if Cupid had lifted his bow and shot him with an arrow. Daytime and nighttime, he was missed by us.

I was younger than Cole when my daddy stepped into my room after everybody was sleeping in bed and kissed my forehead. There was a big yellow moon out the window. I opened my eyes and he was bending over me, his mouth just lifted from my brow. He had his coat on. He put his finger to my lips to shush me. He touched a wisp of my hair, smoothed it away from my face. A moonbeam lit his suitcase on the floor.

"Bye, Daddy," I said.

"Take care of yourself," he whispered. I think his hand was already on the door.

He didn't tell my mama or sister that much, and for a long time I felt lucky he'd picked me to say goodbye to.

Fathers are lost all the time. How to hazard a guess where they even went. Why? Some weren't hardly around long enough to begin with that they could be missed. But still it's long enough. How many grown men don't ever get past it, missing fathers they never had? Common to see in prison, same old story cell after cell.

Justice better take off her blindfold and learn nobody's the same. Nobody's got an equal chance fair square with anybody else. Some have the deck stacked against them from almost the start, dealt a losing hand. Childhood shows the man as morning shows the day, I read that once. In the eyes of the law, every man is equal to the next. But character is sewn from the differences — traits and history peculiar to a body stitch it together. My son is more than the worst thing he ever did in his life. Justice can't be allowed to look away, cover her eyes, pretend right and wrong, good and evil don't bleed together in some men's hearts.

NINE

Cole had a gift for drumming. Ellen noticed it first when he was two years old and banging on trash cans to Count Basie records in her backyard. He could play almost any drum part by ear. It's a knack that he's kept his whole life, still bangs sticks on the side of his bunk in prison, makes his own music. Ellen never let her boys watch television and so Cole was with me, maybe he was five by then, when I turned on "I Love Lucy." He couldn't take his eyes off the screen. He loved Desi Arnaz, Lucy's handsome bandleader husband. But he loved Little Ricky even more. They could have been brothers, except Little Ricky's hair was slicked back and he wore dark make-up so he would look Cuban. That boy had a knack too, a gift for playing the drums, congas and timbales, sometimes in a manic solo or a snappy duet with his father, Ricky Ricardo. I know my son wished he had a family like theirs, musical and funny.

I had this idea to transform the living room into an exotic nightclub a la The Coconut Grove or Bamboo Lounge, The Copacabana. I bought some potted palm trees and changed the light bulbs to glow sultry pink and orange. I set a little table and chairs off to the side, fixed tropical drinks in pineapples garnished with fruit and flowers. When I heard Cole coming up the front steps, home from kindergarten, I put on

Ricky Ricardo's best song, "Babaloo." I could tell I was flushed, overheated even in my sleeveless cocktail dress. I lost count of the layers of red lipstick I rolled on waiting.

You should have seen his face. His expression, if I'd taken a picture, when he saw the new set of used drums I got for him. I didn't need a camera then or now because the picture is clear in my mind. At first Cole just hovered behind the little stool without even picking up the drumsticks. I was worried, waiting to see what he'd do. Then he sat down, looked at me over top a shining cymbal, and started to play. He just played right like that, no doubt in his mind to jinx his rhythm, played to what he heard. His arms flew, unleashed from hanging at his side like birds beating wild, up above clouds. To my ear it sounded faultless and it did touch heaven, lifted us higher than where we were.

I would have bet my last dollar then on Cole having a bright future. It was a good time. I don't know where my son's ability came from, which is why they call it a gift, I guess. It was a gift. Something free and easy nobody had to work for. Natural ability. I could have watched Cole play and never gotten tired of it. I stirred my drink with my finger, sipped sweet rum punch from out of the pineapple then I was kicking step, a conga line of one. Maybe the decorated living room was a pretend setting but our happiness was real. That was a happy day for us.

There were some of those happy times. I add them up, strokes of fortune, blessings each. I wonder the mother I could have been to another child. If Cole had let me, I'd gladly have heaped on some extra hugging and kissing he didn't allow. A baby girl might have cozied with me, found a harbor in my arms. How to know? Child to child, reactions vary to any event. Two brothers witness a car wreck, one is haunted by it all his waking days, the other boy forgets in time it ever happened. If

Cole had had brothers and sisters, they might have tempered our relations. I wonder the difference it would have made to us both. But he was my only child, and I was his only mama, and didn't neither of us get a chance to ever sample anything else. We had to just make out on our own the best we could.

Strange how minor-seeming things can blow up and cause havoc where there was none. Cole had a sweet tooth, hardly worth mentioning, except it was a warning sign I should have paid closer attention to. From the age of three he would wake in the night and rummage through the kitchen cupboards for sugary snacks to sate his craving. He did it at Ellen's, and he did it still when I gathered him back to me. He would eat whatever he could find, cookies, cake, frosting, candied breakfast cereals, chocolate he loved.

I'd hear him drag the metal stool scraping across the floor and then the cupboard doors banged open and closed. He didn't even try to be quiet and I think it was because he didn't half know what he was doing. I should have seen then he'd get taken over by the wanting of something. It took him over.

I liked to bake, it was cooking still but it had the feel of luxury to me, simple decadence. It got so I couldn't keep sweet fixings in the house anymore, not icing sugar or rainbow sprinkles, else they had to be hid where Cole wouldn't hunt. He ate his meals, I made sure that wasn't it, hunger. He had a bedtime snack so he'd go to sleep full and not wake in the night roused by empty pains in his belly. This wasn't any usual hunger. It wasn't normal the way Cole scrounged like a starving tomcat in the dark hours.

I'd find him in the stark electric light of the kitchen, an empty bag of cookies beside him, raiding the cupboards for more. He had shadows under his eyes and he did look hungry, his eyes did.

"What are you doing?" I'd ask him.

He might look at me blankly, pause for a moment. Or he might keep digging so far back in a cupboard he was practically inside it. I'd have to haul him out.

"It's late," I'd tell him. "You have to wait for breakfast now." More than once I'd push him out of the kitchen, get him back settled, tucked in for sleep. I'd just close my eyes and hear him again, opening and closing cupboard doors. His craving dragged him from the comfort of his bed, called him maybe unwilling, but he was called. That he was already a junkie — then it was for sugar, later he became addicted to other substances, drugs, alcohol, he chased with a gnawing, constant appetite — I didn't hardly see. Hope lets slide a good many things, because if you don't make them problems, maybe they won't become that.

Sometimes all there was for Cole to find, pushed way to the back of a shelf, be a box of unsweetened baking chocolate. Expecting it to taste sweet as real milk chocolate, he'd take a bite from a bar. Then when he discovered it wasn't what he wanted, deprived of the sugar-candy taste, he'd throw it down. In the morning I'd find lumps of chocolate spit out and hardened to the counter and the floor. That went on. Even when Cole must have known, he knew the baking chocolate didn't have the flavor he craved, he still opened the wrapped bars and took bites out of them. He ate from each piece in the box, crazy for a fix, as though one piece apart from the others might be what he was after, the gold he was panning for. He doggedly took a bite out of every one. The waste made me just as crazy.

He didn't listen to my chastising. Telling him he had to control himself didn't translate into anything Cole could use. His body spoke another language, I guess, more urgent than plain words. It spoke louder than I did. I thought if he tried harder to fight his impulses this would be a stage he'd outgrow and leave behind. Just a little boy in baggy pajamas dotted with airplanes and sailboats, barely awake, but with a compulsion so fierce, unhealthy, it scared me. Time after time, I'd rise in the morning to tidy the litter from the night before. Then I'd had enough. I waited on him.

I was sitting at the kitchen table drinking a cup of coffee. I'd left the wrappers right where they'd been flung during the night instead of wiping the surface clean the way I usually did, as if what happened then in the dark of night had nothing to do with the light of day. But this was a circle snaking closed on itself.

"Morning," Cole said, rubbing the sand from his eyes, his hair mussed.

I steeled my gaze at him. "Sleep well?" I asked him. He caught something in the breeze of my voice made him lift his head, uneasy. Danger in the wind. He stood still. I told him, "Seems a mouse got into our cupboards last night."

His eyes shot to the mess of chocolate and scattered wrappers, looking obscene and out of place. I saw they looked like news to him. But I was in already, this couldn't go on.

"You know that's baking chocolate?" I told him. "It's meant to be used for cooking. Not to eat the way you eat candy. It's for baking. We've been down this road before but you don't get it. Do you think it's magic? It'll turn sweet just because you want it to? You keep trying it, then spitting it out like it's poison. You can't change it into something it's not. It won't happen."

I looked at him. He looked back, and he was listening, but it was like I was talking about somebody else, not him.

I said, "You know what I think? You never had enough to decide once and for all you don't like the bitter taste."

"Naw," he said.

"You need to try more," I said. "Then you'll know, you like it or you don't."

I took a bar from the counter, unwrapped it fully. "Here."

Cole stepped back away from me and I reached for him, got hold of his pajama sleeve. He tried to make a run from the kitchen but I had him caught, set him down hard in a chair. His shoulders felt slight under my hands, narrow and thin, it gave me pause. I would as soon have put my arms around him. He was struggling to get away but I kept him there, crammed the bittersweet chocolate in his mouth. He was bobbing his head but I was able to get some in, covered my hand across his lips so he couldn't spit out. He tried kicking to scrabble away but I shoved more chunks of chocolate in between his teeth.

"Good?" I asked him. "Sweet? Or is it bitter?"

He sputtered, tears rolled down his cheeks, as mad at being locked in place. Then he gagged, choking. I took my hand from his mouth and hit him on the back. He coughed, coughed until he puked. Tear after tear streamed from his eyes like rain. I poured him a glass of water from the tap, set it on the table near him, but he knocked it over with his arm, fled the room, the chair crashed as it fell back. Those baggy pajamas with the sailboats last thing I saw running from me.

The morning sun shone in the window and I put my face in my trembling hands, blocked it out. My heart was thumping in my chest. Tiny pinpricks of light floated in the blackness behind my eyelids, stars I wished on. After a long while I got to my feet, cleaned the countertops so they gleamed.

Cole stayed in his room, wouldn't come out to eat lunch, wouldn't speak to me or answer to his name when I went to his door. I didn't try to go in. Sometimes he put a chair under the doorknob so it wouldn't open anyway. Dinner came and he stayed in his room. I picked at the food on my plate, fooling it around with my fork. Finally, I called Ellen in tears, told her the thing I had done.

"Sounds like tough love to me," she said. "As a method, it's supposed to work."

"Wasn't but bullying," I told her. "I ought to be ashamed. I am ashamed." I rambled, sorry-hearted. "His nature seems twinned, split good and bad, and you can't punish the one without risk hurting the other. Hurting the other worse."

"He can be an angel when he wants. But how often is that? Maybe boys will be boys. Why not let him come here a couple three days? We're going fishing. We can get an extra rod for Cole and he can come along, give you a break."

"I don't intend giving him up again, Ellen. It's not that I can't handle it." I was at a loss to explain. "It's just hard," I said.

Ellen sighed. "Don't be so sensitive, baby pie. I just meant get him outside — around the boys and fish. Outdoor recreation, that's all."

"Is it a lack of love, do you think that's what makes Cole hunt out sweetness in the dark of night? Some lack spurs him to prowl?"

"Who knows, but I'll tell you this. That boy needs to be saved from himself. He doesn't know what's good for him. He's going to get himself hurt or in trouble. I bet that much. He'd try anybody's patience at times. I swear you never knew what he'd get up to. He has a wild streak, Grace. Just a second."

I heard Ellen cover the phone with her hand, say something muffled, probably to one of her boys. Then clearly, "Go on now. Shoo."

"I never told you this," she came back to me, "but when Cole was living here, he dropped the dog off the roof of the toolshed. Broke both its front legs. Then as if that wasn't bad enough, he hid it inside the shed so nobody'd find it, I think hoping it would die. But it was whimpering so loud I heard it."

I couldn't answer. I was thinking Cole must have been only

three or four then. What was he doing on top of her shed? "Did you see him do that?"

"Well, no. I didn't see him do it. Do you think I would have let him drop the dog if I did? I knew you wouldn't believe it, that's why I didn't say anything before. But just because you don't believe he could do a thing like that, doesn't mean he didn't do it."

I was quiet. The dark truth was I could believe it. "Oh Ellen," I said. "Cole gets up in the night, he stalks around opening cupboards, but I swear if you show him proof in the morning, it scares him. I think something comes on him and he can't help himself. I don't know what. I don't know why. And I'm sure he doesn't either."

"Then you better look out for him, you better do what needs to be done to take care of him. You can't afford a power failure. If Cole can't watch out for himself, you better see the way lit to do it yourself. I tied his leg to the crib at night. For his own protection. Children can't wander lost in the dark. I couldn't have him going through everything in my kitchen, what if he ate poison? Cut himself on a knife? What if he bled to death on my floor? Nights are not meant for children. Kids need sunshine like flowers."

"You tied him to the bed?"

"Well so?"

"Ellen, you tied him so he couldn't get up?"

"It's not like I used iron shackles. A pair of old pantyhose, soft as those get after a few washings. I didn't use a leather leash or a length of chain, or rope. He was tied soft. Jesus, Grace. Hasn't some lover tied you to the bed that way? It's no big deal."

The thought of my son tied by his leg, bound to his bed. I hated myself for ever giving him up, not keeping him under my care. I hated Ellen. I hated the thing in Cole, whatever it was, made him act the way he did. But now years later, I wonder. Was it so wrong? That is bald honesty. I wonder if it wasn't wrong to cut him loose, let him face harm. Let him do harm.

As he grew, I gave Cole a weekly allowance he used to buy candy. It never lasted him longer than a blink, and after it was gone, he stole. I found a stash of Heath bars under his mattress. At first he told me they weren't his and he couldn't figure how they came to be there. He shook his head in puzzlement. Then, why was I snooping under his bed? he wanted to know. He always had an answer. He guessed one of his friends must have secretly hid them, forgot and gone home. He never would say — *This thing I did, Mama, this thing you know I did, it's my fault. I did it.* He wouldn't shoulder a blame, come clean and move on.

Every day after the school bell went, a bunch of the kids jangled into Tucker's Variety and then not long after spilled out again with paper bags of candy. It must have seemed easy to Cole to take what he wanted without being seen or paying for it. He just had to slip full hands into deep pockets and come up innocent, empty again. He wouldn't have thought twice whether it be the right thing, or the wrong. Just it was easy. I bet he'd pride himself on it. But Cole pushed the odds, did it so often he was bound to get caught.

To try to make amends, I had him return the candy I'd found under the bed, take it back to the store and face up to it. He said he paid for all those chocolate bars out of his allowance. "This is dumb," he said.

I put them into a sack and marched with him and watched him do it. I stood in the doorway while Cole sauntered to the teenage girl behind the counter and handed her over the bag. He said something to her, she was pretty, taller than him, and she tilted her head. She got a kind of funny look, curious. Cole said something else and he leaned in towards her smiling. What was he then, twelve maybe? She peered into the sack, bent and put it behind the counter somewhere. She gave him a little shrug of her shoulders then slanted her eyes my way, and she and Cole shared a joke while looking at me. That was it.

Cole walked over to the door. Not with his head low, humbled, swaggered out past me, even as the girl had her hand still raised in a cute goodbye wave he didn't bother to catch but I did. Girls always liked him. Girls and women both. He had a way of bringing them out of their shells, let them show off the sweet mother side, and their sexier musky flip side. Not many could resist the urge to baby him into a man, in doing that feel themselves somewhere near whole.

It was gone a year after that the new owner of Tucker's called me on the phone, told me he'd caught my son shoplifting. Again. He said, *again*. He wanted me to come down there so we could talk about it, iron it out, decide what to do. He said he'd warned Cole before and now had a mind to report him to the police. It was but candy not big cash dollars, but still he said, the thieving was regular and it added up. A drop in the bucket eventually floods over, makes a mess. He didn't want to prosecute, he let the word hang, but Cole wasn't leaving him any choice. I hardly heard all he said after, for the blood pounding in my ears. I could only tell him, a weak whisper, I was on my way. He'd wait for me inside and wouldn't let Cole go until I came.

I switched out of my dress and into a fresh other one, neatened my hair, French-twisted it at the back. It was so hot. Summertime, school was about to end. I opened the fridge and stood for a minute inside its mouth, letting the cold breath lick across my skin. I took a bag of frozen peas from the freezer and held it on the nape of my neck. Sometimes I kept my panties chilled in the fridge but that day I left them off altogether. It was too hot for layers of clothing. As soon as I closed the door again, the heat hit full on, and I felt myself get damp with it. The store wasn't far, not a long walk, but the pavement burned up through my sandals so I ended by carrying them in my hand, walking barefoot on the grass beside the road.

June flowers were in bloom and practically every house I passed had a hanging basket brimming with fuchsias or azaleas on its porch, wisteria draped doorways, roses massed walls. I felt then the way I do when I see the beds of pretty flowers outside the prison. They hit me like a slap. Some things are too beautiful for where they are, or maybe for where you are in your mind. And it hurts, bothersome as a thorn slivered under your skin.

Tucker's was an old wood-shingled building with a railed front veranda and ornate screened door, the mesh torn and ripped from careless use. I slipped my feet back into my sandals, bending to buckle the sides, and when I looked up I saw Cole. He was wearing a canvas apron, lifting bottles of soda from a crate and setting them down into a large Coca-Cola cooler that was outside on the veranda next to the door. I walked towards him, watching as he picked the bottles up by their necks, two in each hand, and placed them into the cooler, bent again to the crate.

"Cole?" I called as I neared.

He straightened and turned, wiping his forehead with his arm. He was clearly surprised to see me. He didn't look troubled, not at all. He leaned over, put the last bottles into the cooler then banged the lid shut and kicked the empty crate sliding out of the way with his foot.

"Guess what?" he said to me, coming down the steps every other one and jumping off the third last to the ground.

Before I could answer, he pulled a handkerchief from his shirt pocket, a dark cloud scudding across his eyes. "You're red as a beet, Mama. You better step into the shade."

I took the square of cotton, passed it over my face. It smelled like Cole and I held onto it.

"Mr. Naylor, he owns Tucker's now, he gave me a job." Cole hadn't let up watching me with worriment and now he bounded back up the stairs, dug a frosty Coke from the bottom of the cooler. He pried the metal cap off with his teeth and handed me the bottle. "Take a big swallow."

The liquid seared my throat but it was welcome all the same.

"Better?" he said.

I nodded.

"He gave me a job. Since I was in here hanging around all the time, Mr. Naylor said I might as well be working for him. Gave me this apron to put on."

Just then a man came out of the store onto the screened veranda, paused at the doorway leading down the stairs. The old door was fixed open with a cast-iron jam. He reached up and took hold of the top of the doorframe with his fingertips, settled there with a knee bent, gazing down on us. Posed in the doorway, casual. He had gray hair, the kind that comes on early and looks handsome, better even than hair that still keeps its color. He was dressed in jeans and boots, a tight white T-shirt with an eagle printed on it.

Cole said, "Mr. Naylor. This here's my mama, sir."

He came down the steps. "Ma'am," he said. He squinted deep-set eyes at the light of day, lines creasing the tan of his skin. He pushed his hand back through his hair. He spoke slow and to me, shutting Cole from the frame of his vision. "I caught your boy stealing, that's the long and short of it. I've seen him do it before, more than one time, and I warned him about it. Didn't I, son?" He was looking at me still. "Like I told you on the phone, it adds up. Take that apron off, boy."

Cole glanced from Naylor to me, startled. I could tell he

didn't know what was going on. No matter what he'd done that didn't seem right. He looked back at Naylor. Then seeing it wasn't a joke, he struggled out of the apron, pulling it off hard over his head. For just an instant, he held it crushed between his hands before he gave it up, thrust it at Naylor.

"Now empty your pockets. Show your mama what's in there."

Cole edged back. He shoved his hands down into his pockets and left them. "You called my mama on the phone? You told her to come here?"

I knew I ought to say something, I wanted to. I pressed the cold bottle to my flaming cheek.

The man took hold of Cole's wrist and pulled his hand out of his pocket. He stuck his own into the opening and dug up a candy bar and a rope of licorice. Cole was tugging away, not making it easy. Still the man got his hand down into the bottom of the other pocket and came up with some loose change.

"I was going to pay for the stuff," Cole said. "That money's proof I was." He looked like being touched had laid cooties on him, crawly under his skin.

Naylor bounced the change in his palm. "Every day you come into my store and steal from me. Even if you could pay, you'd rather just take what you want. That costs the other kids who have to pay more because of you. You can't get something for nothing. Life doesn't work that way."

Cole sneered. "Take the money. I just forgot to pay is all."

The man dropped the change on the ground and moved his boot over it. We all watched the shining silver get covered in dirt.

"Cole," I spoke up, "you're lucky Mr. Naylor didn't call the police. You ought to thank him for that. Tell him you won't forget to buy your candy again."

Cole frowned at me slightly, didn't say anything.

"Well?" I said.

"What?"

"You're sorry. Tell him."

Cole said nothing. Then he looked up at Naylor. "Why'd you give me a job? You told me to put on that apron and help out."

"You're going to pay me back something of what you owe in labor. I told you. You don't get nothing for nothing. Get on uncrating those bottles, while I talk to your mama inside."

"That ain't no job. What a gyp. You're not paying me a wage. It's not fair. That's slavery."

"There's your money, boy." Naylor kicked at the change in the dust with the toe of his boot. We all stood looking down. "Uncrate those boxes, hear?" he said.

"Or what?" Cole said.

"Son," I said, trying to warn him with my eyes, he better go on.

"Don't even dare bend my ear about fair. Or I promise you I'll call the cops."

"He'll do it," I said. "Go on, Cole," I urged him.

The store was only marginally cooler inside than it was outside, the air pushed around by a wobbly ceiling fan. The light fixtures weren't on and it took my eyes a while to adjust to the relative darkness. I took a long swig from the bottle of Coke.

"Jim Naylor," the man said and shook my hand as if we were only meeting now. He smiled but there was something in it I didn't like. Scorn, pity, I couldn't tell just what was it.

"Grace," I said.

"You raising that boy on your own, Grace?"

"I'm raising him and he's raising hell, I guess."

He smiled some more, less fake. "You got your work cut out."

He leaned back against the counter. We were the only ones in the store. I could hear the faint clink of glass bottles as Cole loaded them into the cooler. Naylor said, "My wife is a religious woman, Grace. With our boys she always quoted Proverbs: 'Train up a child in the way he should go and when he is old, he will not depart from it.'"

"There's a line for everything, seems."

"Does seem," he agreed. "If you know the Scriptures good enough you can back up any argument. My wife can. I never won an argument with her yet. She's a fanatic." His eyes held mine. He reached out and put his finger to the indent above my lip, pressed gently. "You're so pretty," he said. It had a hush of wonderment to it. "You even look pretty when you sweat."

"I do?" I whispered. I kept just still.

He laughed, his eyes still lingering on mine. "Yes you do, Grace. It makes me want to kiss you. Can I kiss you?" He touched a strand of my hair. I turned away slightly, the ceiling fan spinning above me off kilter.

"I want to show you something," he said. He led me into a messy little room behind a door marked Private. "Look." He pointed to a sheet of paper on his desk. I saw right away what it was. A record of Cole's shoplifting, a list of dates and what he'd taken. A long list. "I could call the police," he said. "Maybe I should."

I had my back to him, leaning over the desk to read the scrawled writing. I turned and looked at him over my shoulder.

"But now we've met, Grace, I'm glad I called you." He smiled. Then he put his hand on my behind, moved it slowly down the curve.

I kept my back to him, closed my eyes. He made a sound when he discovered I had no panties on. He traced the line between my buttocks with the edge of his finger, lightly, slowly. Then he gathered the fabric of my dress, bunching it up at the sides, raising it higher. I felt it lifting, licking the backs of my thighs like lapping water and I didn't move. It took ages. When he reached around and cupped my breast, pinched the nipple until it was hard between his fingers, I felt it with relief.

He turned me then to face him and he unbuttoned my dress, let it fall to the floor. He looked at me fully naked before putting his mouth to the tip of my breast, nibbling at the other nipple, pulling on it until they both stood erect. He knelt in front of me, admiring the symmetry, then trickled his finger down my belly to touch the curls of pubic hair and lower to a slit barely visible. He dipped his finger into the wet depth and made another sound. He leaned his head against my thigh. "You want this," he said in a low voice.

I did then. It was like a fever. It was like I was riding a wave, riding it, to break foaming on the shore. At the touch of his lips, his hot tongue opening my vagina, I shuddered and let out my breath, that fast. He put his finger back inside me to feel the pulsing all around it. He stood, kissing my stomach, my breast, my shoulder, then he unzipped his jeans. He pushed me gently down on the desk and had me urgently, holding my hips, looking at the wall.

Cole was sitting on the veranda steps drinking a Coke when I came out.

"What were you doing?" he said. "Mama?"

I walked on and he came after me, running to catch up.

"I was going to pay for that candy," he said, but he didn't try too hard to mean it.

He took my hand in his, which he never did, and we walked home that way. Most clearly I remember the heat, holding hands with my son while he drank an ice-cold Coke he didn't pay anybody for.

NOCTURNAL ANIMALS

Nocturnal animals live shrouded in darkness, a world of night. They are photophobic by nature, although some will approach the light. This willingness seems to depend on whether they are a predator or prey species. Nocturnal creatures like rats or mice, afraid of light, tend to be prey species. They are protein converters, their role in the food chain is to be eaten. In danger, their response is to run for cover and hide. Wolves and coyotes, technically nocturnal species, are predators. Driven by want and past experience, they will risk exposure and venture into the light to find a good meal.

TEN

I sat looking up at Jupiter, the black dog lying in the dandelions at my feet, us both lulled by the swooning opera of night bugs. Nearly midnight. Time was a slow hand moving over the face of my watch. Long slow seconds, endless minutes. How many years would Cole draw for this if he got caught? How many years of his life did he use up in that instant he stuck the guard with that metal rod and ran? Years in prison, doing time, a whole other thing than telling time by the clock, or passing time, or killing time. And the guard. Not forget about him. Time lost off his life too — blood, trust. More, hope. Not ever forget about him. And if Cole gets to Ivy, what about her? Soon I'll walk into the woods to meet my son, then what about me? Time is something Cole and I kept track of between us, it's always been amongst us.

In the jail during visits they'd cut your time short, cancel it out when you got all the way there, tell you come back another day, but they'd never let you have a minute extra, wouldn't give you any longer than they were required to. As if they couldn't wait to bust it up and haul the men, put them back in their cells. Cole wasn't the only one easy to set off, somebody just had to look at him the wrong way. His moods swung wild.

Sometimes his tears fell, taking him by surprise. All those men down, their emotions rubbed raw, doesn't take much till they shoot off, explode. A visit can be acid on them at times, seeing their family.

I'd tell Cole a story, some recollection from when he was coming up, or maybe show him a picture I'd found. I remember I brought in to show him the memory book hospitals used to give new mothers. You recorded your child's first word, first step, first baby song, or toy he liked. It went from birth to five years, had adorable drawn illustrations on each page and lines to fill in. Cole's book ended with his first haircut when he was two, before I took him to stay at Ellen's. I kept a lock of his hair in the book. That was the last thing I recorded, how I cut his hair myself, a white towel around his shoulders. I sat him in the kitchen and gave him a sucker to bribe him to keep still, cut as fast as I could. The hair was soft and dark, curled sweetly, the tape holding it to the page yellowed.

I flipped through the empty pages came after that, though usually I didn't let myself look long at what I missed with him. I thought Cole would see how much he was loved, proof he was precious to me, I'd paid attention to each tooth as it grew in his mouth. But he cared more about those blank pages than anything else. All the small triumphs and accomplishments of his early childhood that went unrecorded. It was as though they'd never happened, they weren't remarkable. As though the pages of his life were blank too, meant nothing.

Cole got choked by it and I was sorry I ever thought it would be nice to show him. We took a pause. It's hard to see your son with hands cuffed, but harder, I couldn't dab his tears away, had to watch him bend his head, raise all that steel just to wipe his eye. In that pause when neither of us said anything, you'd hear it. The roar. Time running out. Not a lighter sound like you might think, sand drifting through an hourglass, no. We'd take a wait, the talk dried up, and I'd glance at my watch. My eyes would fix there in shock. Only five minutes left.

Five minutes but then a whole week until I would see him again. That roar would drown out my son's next few words. I'd know he was trying to make a bridge, throw a rope across a canyon to get to me so I had to hear him. I'd look up and see his mouth moving. The roar made me dizzy. I didn't want to miss a word my son said, plain and simple as his language could be, it mattered I hear it. He was making an effort to talk to me. I had to fight to block everything out but him. Then all sudden I would hear him again. Hear him and nothing else. Music to my ears, the sound of his voice. I'd know what he was saying. "I hear you, son," I'd say.

The black dog stretched and rolled onto his side, his legs shuddering in a dream. I was judging him to be slothful since the more at ease he got with me, the more he just laid prone so I had to step over him to get places. I stood up and he lifted his head, his eyes barely opened.

"Stay, you lazybones," I told him, as if I needed to.

I started walking towards the towering trees at the far end of the yard, looking back to see if the dog was trying to come after me, I had him chained. "Stay," I told him again even though he was doing that, hadn't bothered to get up. "I'll be back," I said to hear my voice, hear out loud I'd be coming back. He watched me, a locked shadow, lightning bugs glinting in the air above him. I crossed my arms over my chest. The woods seemed a solid wall.

It was a clear night, bold moon and no shy stars. I thought of a picture Cole had drawn and given me once, a night like this. Clear, a big sky dashed with long white needles of light. The flaring trails of a meteor shower. Streaks of light like rain. He drew himself at the bottom, arms wide open as if to embrace all the shooting stars. Or as if the stars were birds, and he'd opened his arms and let them slash the sky with perfect flight.

A few yards into the trees a curtain fell and it went black. I had to watch my footing, taking blind baby steps with my hands shielding back branches. There was a dank smell, decaying plants, earth. I thought I could find my way to the stump though it had been years. It was a place Cole used to hide and play, spent a lot of time there until at nightfall I'd come bring him home, scared of him being orphaned after dark. I remember I came on him nestled sound sleeping on a bed of moss like a wood sprite, dirty bare feet, soft wispy hair. When I got closer I saw he had a spider bite on his forehead. I imagined the spider with its long legs crawling over his cheek, crossing the bridge of his nose, climbing the pale slope of his brow. I shook him to get up, pulled him standing before he was even awake.

I couldn't see the sky anymore, no hint of moon. The wind was breathing through the trees, panting like it was chasing me. I faltered. It was just as dark behind me as it was in front. "Cole?" I wasn't far enough yet I knew, knew he couldn't hear me. I didn't want to go on, further into the tangled underbrush, the trees menacing over me. I blinked to try to see better this shadow from that. I took a step, and another. I thought of the night Cole was born, how I had to push through the pain if I wanted to hold him in my arms. If I ever wanted to see his face.

I never did like walking in the dark, not seeing the ground at my feet. It reminded me of the house of horrors when the fair came to town. The floor tilted and quaked beneath me, skeletons jerked from their coffins rattling their bones, cobwebs broke clinging to hair. Once Cole came with me and he ran through the twisting corridors while I stumbled after him, his footsteps fading fast.

I made it to the tree stump and in the wan light, because now the moon just barely broke through the topmost branches, I saw the ground was stubbed with cigarette butts, the empty bottle of sour mash whiskey laying there. Rainwater had pooled in a dent in the earth, slick and shining. I heard Cole before I saw him, heard him singing in a low, gravelly voice.

"Froggy went a'courtin' and he did ride. Um hmm. Um hmm. With a sword and a pistol by his side."

"Cole?"

He came from out of the trees, twigs snapping under his feet, and stood in the pool of water.

"You're going to be soaked now," I said. "Look it, you're wet." He bent his head stared dumbly at his shoes, pitching forward and staggering a clumsy step. I took his arm, pulled him to where it was dry.

He sang, "Well, he rode on down to Miss Mousey's door where he had been so many times before. Um hmm."

"You're drunk on that whiskey," I stated as fact.

He had sunglasses on, now at midnight, two silver mirrors instead of eyes. I saw my own face when I looked at him. It was what Ivy must have seen too, on her wedding day, because he wore a like pair of mirrored shades all through the ceremony. He was stoned, still high from the night before, and the smoking he did on his way to the church so he wouldn't come down. Ivy said I do, and must have gazed deep into her own eyes, making herself a promise that was no reflection on him. She watched herself vow those words, gave herself a determined little smile and closed her eyes, leaning in to kiss him, not expecting more than a cold reception. Maybe it cheered her when his lips at least said I do back.

"He took Miss Mousey on his knee and asked her, Miss Mousey will you marry me?" Cole put a cigarette in his mouth and struck a match, it flared bright, dimmed as fast and he shook it out. "The owl did hoot and the birds did sing and all through the woods the music rang."

"Quit," I said. "And take those sunglasses off so I can talk to you." When he didn't, I reached to take them off him myself, but he dashed his head away.

"Well, what will the wedding breakfast be?"

"Please stop," I said.

"Two green beans and a black-eyed pea."

He took a long drag on the cigarette. I waited. He took another, sitting on the stump, seeming lost in thought.

"Son?" I said.

"I'm in real deep shit, Mama."

"I know. I'm scared."

"You think you're scared now —" he said, breaking off.

"I want to ask you again. I want to see your eyes. Please take off those sunglasses."

"The eyes are the window to your soul," he said, mocking a joke out of what I said. "Don't you get it? There's nothing to see, Mama. I don't have no soul."

But he took the glasses off. He turned his eyes to me then, and in that instant they caught the moonlight, glowed with fire. My heart missed a beat and my hand flew to my chest.

"Ha," he smirked. "I told you. I'm the boogeyman. Welcome to my nightmare."

"It's just the way the light's catching you," I said.

"Do you know what I see when I look at you, Mama?"

"No."

Whatever he was going to say, he didn't then. His neck drooped and he buried his face in his arms as if hiding from the pictures in his head. When he spoke it was muffled. "Something real bad has happened and I can't tell you what."

"I know already. The jail guard."

"Fuck the guard." Cole bolted upright with the words, his back rigid. "Fuck him." He pulled a blade of wet grass and chewed it. "I'm dying of thirst," he said, as if to himself. "What were those berries you told me about, Mama? You only had to eat three of them and it would kill you. Some weed, was it?"

"Deadly nightshade. Belladonna."

"I could use a handful. I guess you don't have any of those little cherries with you?"

I shook my head.

"Anyway I know you wouldn't give them to me, but you could tell me where they're at. I'll get them myself. I bet they're pretty as candy."

"Cole? What's happened?"

"I got to have some water." He was staring down at the puddle, the gloss of its surface dead smooth. The smoke from his cigarette rose thinly from his hand.

"That water's full of fever," I said.

He kept staring at it, seeming to consider whether to drink of it, if it was worth the risk.

"Cole? You've made some mistakes. But you only need another chance to prove —"

"To prove what, Mama? What do you think I'm going to prove?"

"Listen. Should I call your lawyer? Are you planning to give yourself up? I'm here to help you."

He smirked. "Naw. That ain't the plan, no sir. That is not what I'd like you to do." He fumbled in his shirt pocket, took out a scrap of paper. "I called Ivy and she's waiting for me at this motel." He passed me the paper. "I'm going there to try work it out with her. I need you to rent us a place, maybe an hour or so away, somewhere we can hole up. A dive, nothing special. Then you call us at the motel." He tossed his cigarette into the water so it rippled the satin sheen with a hiss. "Okay?" he said.

I nodded.

"Sure?" he said.

I managed to look at him. I'd been reading the name of the motel over and over, thinking about Jackson and Niagara Falls where Cole's life got started. A motel seems an escape, a safe place to hide out, but only seems. There's no such place. I nodded again.

"Did you bring any money, Mama? I better boot it out of here."

I looked down at my dress that didn't have any pockets even, touched the button at the throat of my sweater. I stammered that I didn't. "I didn't think to," I said. "I'll go back."

"I can't wait for you to go back. Forget it."

"I'm sorry."

"What did you ever do to be sorry for, Mama? Other than having me."

I put my arms around him and he stood for it, stood hard still but he didn't hug back. Just let me hold my boy.

"You can't kiss things better, Mama," he said in my ear, pushing me off then.

He bent down to a sack he'd hid behind the stump. He put the empty whiskey bottle in it and he tugged a steel blade out of the ground where it'd been sticking, hidden by the long grass.

"That's my kitchen knife," I said.

"I had to borrow it." He held the knife in midair then swiped it across his palm, opening a startled red line in his skin.

What would a fortune-teller read now for his future? The map held in the palm of his hand, road of his life, paths he could have taken blurred, all but washed out by blood. "Don't be reckless with yourself," I said.

Cole wrapped a rag around his hand, blood seeping between the cracks of his fingers. He put the knife in the sack.

How many times I'd used that knife and never thought twice about it, never felt dread. He must have taken it when I was packing up the food for him at the house. I hadn't known it was gone.

"Well" — he slid on his sunglasses — "guess I'll go find Miss Mousey, sit her on my knee."

"Be careful," I said.

"Easier to be careful now." He lifted the sack to draw meaning to it, the knife in it. "Won't be no more goddamned baseball bats swinging at my head."

I saw myself in his eyes, staring up at him dumb as a post. "What?" I said.

"Nothing. Just this guy, this fucker. All I wanted was to get some food. I was hungry. I needed some money to get here with, that's all. Just was going to take the money and beat it. I was in the guy's face acting tough, I don't have a weapon, faking I do. He pulls a baseball bat from behind the counter, starts making all this noise. He's yelling, 'Get out! Police!' this bullshit. Waving the bat. I just want to get out. Fuck, I want to get out. But the guy won't shut up. I took the bat off him, asshole, and now he's hollering more. 'Don't hurt me, help, help, God.' I hit him just to shut him up. Shut the fuck up. If I had a knife, wouldn't have happened that way. Blah blah blah, boo hoo. Would've had quiet."

I put my face in my hands so I didn't have to look at myself in his mirrored lenses, made me look so small, shrank me in my own eyes.

"Anyway," he said, "the good thing was he had a truck, keys hanging out his pocket, tank full of gas. It was a shake better than hitching. Mama? I told you it was bad. You asked me. Don't ask, you don't want to know."

I covered my mouth as if my not speaking would stop him from saying the things he'd said. It was as bad as it had ever been, and I knew it wasn't as bad as it would get. I couldn't think of when else Cole had ever told me he'd done something wrong, admitted it flat out. Instead of giving me hope, it scared me. Seemed this was just the last leg of a journey he'd started years before. The route was already cut out, cut in stone. "I don't like being here," I said. "I can't stay."

Cole shrugged. There was a time he wouldn't have wanted to be alone in the dark, and I wouldn't have left him. But this was where he could be. The landscape inside him was somehow this place.

The night came undone. I ran through the tangled net of trees, wild and crashing, ran for the yellow light beckoning through the branches. The light from my kitchen window, shining brighter and brighter, steady, ran until I hit grass, saw the black dog on his feet wagging his tail. I brought him into the house with me, locked the door. I threw off my clothes, stood in a hot shower soaping myself as if I could get clean, as if I wasn't out of breath, as if my heart would ever calm, beat gently again in its bone cage.

My mind was reeling. Every time I let myself think at least Cole was safe, he was free, I thought of him with the baseball bat hitting the clerk, thought of the guard falling to his knees. The sack holding a knife that belonged to me, a whiskey bottle could be broken, wielded, jagged edges cutting like razors.

I dressed in my robe, went to the phone. I could call Ellen, Cole's lawyer, the police. I could. I didn't lift the receiver. I sat like I was stunned, my arms lifeless in my lap. I had to hope Cole would get to Ivy. Hoped she would calm him down, even if I couldn't go near believing it. Ivy didn't have that effect on him. I hoped he'd get back on track, somehow settle into a normal life with normal troubles like everybody else. I had to believe in the promise of a future, the ability to change.

I thought of the polished scarlet berries of the deadly night-shade. They were pretty as candy, Cole was right. I could gather some in a china bowl. For once, I wondered if he shouldn't have what he craved. I would put some in his hand, take some in mine. The burst of poison on my tongue tasting like love to me. I would swallow any bitterness at the end, fill myself with love.

METEORS

Meteor showers happen when pieces of stone and ice race into the Earth's atmosphere at such speed that friction with the air heats them to incandescence. As they burn out and turn to dust, a final flare causes their brilliant trail across the sky. On a clear night, needle-like streaks of light from these shooting stars can be seen, as many as a dozen in an hour. It used to be that shooting stars were associated with souls, and their fall foretold someone's death. But now when a star moves as falling from the sky, a wish is made.

ELEVEN

I tried to keep my hands from resting idle with any number of hobbies over the years, apart from my gardening and baking, reading. I took up knitting and quilting, things I thought I would never do like macrame. I was stitching a needlepoint pillow cover with the motto *Stand Fast Before The Wind,* when I saw a group of women coming up on the doorstep. I knew who they were. Mothers of boys the same age as Cole, he was fifteen, in his classes at school. Boys who should have been his friends and these angry women who might have been mine. Except to them Cole was trouble and they put me in the same boat with him.

I had my head tilted towards the front window to make use of the natural light, since the black yarn was hard on my vision and it was the entire background color. I saw them coming, five of them I counted. Stand fast before the wind. I put down the pillow cover, went and pulled open the door before the rap even came.

The first time they'd stood there — could Cole have been just eight? — I'd asked them to please come in, sit down. I was thinking I'd serve them iced tea in long tall glasses and we'd visit in the living room, chat amongst women. But it wasn't a social call. They stood out on the front steps raising their voices to a shrill pitch, berating me for anybody to hear. Telling me I better do something about my son. I looked from face to face, dredging their eyes for any ray of understanding. There was none. They saw the bewilderment in my gaze, the growing sick dread, the floundering lost look, and it made them angrier still.

"What did he do?" I asked, feeling the fool. I was scorned more for being the last to know.

It set them off, rolling their eyes heavenward, preaching gloomy forecasts. By then, age of eight, Cole already had a bad reputation. He'd been suspended six times for fighting in the schoolyard. The mothers wanted to have him expelled. He'd thrown a tantrum, overturned desks, ripped artwork from the walls, kicked and cussed his teacher. Their children were afraid of him, they said, came home crying, fretted into their pillows at night. They got stomachaches and headaches, didn't want to get on the bus in the morning. The principal was going to bring Cole home and talk to me about a reform school.

I didn't say anything. What could I? I'm sure I gaped, big blank eyeballs, my mouth a fixed O like a fish out of water, strangling on air. I saw those women calling each other on the phone, sharing coffee at each other's kitchen tables, maybe on a shopping spree together for a new outfit, each other's admiring mirrors. Their sons would be best friends, and on weekends, they might take turns sleeping over at the other's houses. They'd put on their pajamas and plunk down in front of the TV, eating pizza and potato chips and popcorn, until it was later than they were usually let be up. They'd make a game out of brushing their teeth, fight each other with their pillows, then climb into sleeping bags and whisper in the dark until one of them asked, *Are you asleep?* and got no answer.

These women knew each other by their first names. They knew husbands' names, and the names of their children's brothers and sisters. They knew the inside pockets of each other's lives, the fabric lining turned inside out. But they didn't know my name. They didn't care to. All who I was — Cole's mother. And his name they tramped on. There on my doorstep, they tramped on it until it was mud.

I looked at some of those same faces now, older, like I was to them. I don't guess, truth be, I saw them for who they were, any more than they saw me as my real self. It was a blur. They accused Cole of selling drugs in the schoolyard, and of showing their sons how to hotwire a car and drive it joyriding. He was making them all delinquents. He was the root of their problems. I sighed, shut my eyes. In my mind I pulled the black yarn through the mesh pattern, stitched a neat cross. It seemed like a lot of Xs but one stitch at a time, it'd get done. Stand fast before the wind. Stitch by stitch.

"Don't think we don't know what's going on with you. We've seen the cops parked outside your house. At least twice. You keep your trouble to yourself," a frazzy redhead stated, her hands on her hips.

"Where's the father anyhow? Maybe he could straighten him out." This from a woman dressed like a child, with puffed sleeves and a peter pan collar.

Cole had lit a neighbor's car on fire, set another fire in somebody's woodshed. He wanted to burn it up with equal zeal Jackson had wanted to fight fires down. Could be it was the same flaming passion, right side and wrong side of the law.

"I'll talk to him when he gets home," I said. I was scuffing my feet in the slippers Cole had given me on my birthday. Slide-on mules I wore daily, mock blue suede. He'd also given me a spray bottle of cologne. I wondered now if he'd stolen them for the occasion. Did I honestly think he'd saved up his money, planned ahead for something to give me and himself done without? I woke up to it then — you can believe what you want, whatever you want, but wishing and hoping, and even believing, don't make a thing true.

"Speak up," somebody said.

"I'll talk to him." I could scarcely lift my eyes. I saw them shaking their heads like it was a lost cause, like I was. Just beyond them, a tiny hummingbird hovered at my sugar-water feeder. Its wings were moving too fast to be seen. Its heart was big in proportion to its body. The tiniest bird had the biggest heart. It would be racing at atomic speed. I wondered what risk was love for a heart like that? The breaking of it more suffering than was fair deserved. But such bliss, while love lasted. I thought I could hear the humming whir of the bird's wings, a live wind-up toy, painted as bright with its ruby throat. The sound of invisible wings beating the air to keep from falling.

"This is a decent neighborhood. Doesn't seem your talking's done any good. Are you listening to us? Why not save your breath? Take a belt to him."

"He's not a child anymore," I said. "He's fifteen."

"She's scared of him," someone muttered. "No wonder."

"I'm just telling you he's tall for his age, and he's strong. Words are all I've got."

A voice hadn't spoken yet said, "Our husbands would be only too happy to cut him down to size for you. They'd hammer the point home."

I heard her threat. I felt the wind, that swirling black wind Cole had been born out of, blow me back into the house, slam the door closed.

By the time he came in, I'd shucked the slippers he'd given me on my birthday with a note signed, *Anyways and always, C.J.* All these years that's the only way he's ever signed a letter or card to me. I was turning the bottle of cologne over in my hands, the glass cool as a stone.

"So?" I said to him.

Cole rummaged in the fridge then chugged orange juice from the carton. "So what?" He set to making a sandwich at the table. Food mattered to him, have it just how he cared for it, like bread slices be kept whole not cut across the middle, or he wouldn't eat unless with chopsticks, that after we saw a kung fu movie at the drive-in.

"Those women, that group of mothers came here again."

He banged the peanut butter jar down, licked the knife clean.

"Don't do that, you'll injure your tongue. Plus it's rude."

He stuck the knife in the jar.

"That's as bad," I said. "You just had that knife all over your mouth. Now your germs are in the peanut butter. I wish you'd think about bacteria."

"What did they want?" Cole rubbed his jaw, a habit he'd launched since dark hairs had started to grow on his chin. He'd be asking for a razor to shave soon. Sometimes I caught him gazing at his image in the bathroom mirror. Whenever he looked at himself, he squared his shoulders and beefed himself up, trying to make the mirror reflect the way he saw himself, bigger than his years, so close to being a man he could touch it.

"Germs aren't funny," I said. "Maybe you think they are, but they're not."

"What are you talking about?"

"Germs."

"Why?"

"I want you to know they're nothing to laugh at. You can't see them but they cause trouble. Germs have got a life of their own. They're out there." I wagged my head, pointed at him. "You're reckless."

"Me?" he said.

"Who else?"

"I don't know. Germs?"

"We're talking about your manners. And those women on the porch calling names."

"They should leave you alone."

"They do. They would never come near me if they could help it."

Cole took a bite out of the sandwich. "Stupid bitches."

"They said you've been selling drugs. Teaching their boys how to hotwire cars."

"You believe them?"

"There it is. That's what they said."

"Do you believe them?"

I looked at my son. I watched him chewing his food, the dimple in his cheek. Child of mine. It comes down to this: *You believe them?* out of my boy's mouth. Do I, don't I — does it make a difference if I do, or not? To him, or to me? This is my child, my only child I'll ever have, that's what I know.

I remember when Mama was dying, and I'd called the ambulance to come and take her to the hospital at the end, I'd dressed her and we waited for them in the kitchen. She sat in a chair and I stood with my arm around her shoulders. Her chin trembling, she said, "I won't see my kitchen again." It was all she could get out, any more and she'd cry and her intent was to be brave. The cold, hateful truth of it. She wouldn't see her kitchen again. She was on her way dying. The truth won't always set you free. It'll pin you down and hold you there, not let you move. All I did, squeeze her shoulders because she'd spoken the mean truth out loud, faced it square on, we both knew she had. But I said, "You will too." Only thing I could, look at the truth and lie to it, goddamn it to hell. Did it make things easier? Or nicer? When it came down to the words being spoken, nothing was easy.

I said, "They just want their boys to get on through high school, graduate, and have futures ahead of them. It's the same as I want for you."

"Give it up, Mama. Soon as I hit sixteen, I'm dropping out, I promise you that. I'd like to see those old bags show proof of what they say I did."

I took the gold lid off the bottle of cologne and misted my neck. "This was a nice present. It meant a lot to me on my birthday. And the slippers too."

Cole did kind of a double take. Maybe he thought I'd tell him he couldn't quit school. I'd tell him not to sell drugs, or don't steal cars. "I could get you another bottle for Christmas," he said, "if it's used up."

"You stole them."

His face flushed. "I did not."

"How much did they cost then?"

"I don't remember."

"You don't know," I said.

"They were a gift, you're not supposed to ask." He stood so his chair scraped back. "You're not supposed to ask, Mama. They were for you."

"You stole them."

"I did not." He said each word on its own, giving it space. His hand curled into a fist and he drew his arm in ready to throw a punch. He stared at me, unwavering, with hard eyes.

"You're a good actor," I said, but I was holding myself braced. He swung, not at me, at the last second not at me, but the wall caving in a hole, then he ran out.

I sat brooding and the conviction descended on me that I couldn't accuse my boy. Wasn't somewhere the thought good, to get me a gift on my birthday? The stealing was wrong, but the thought behind was pure. Not that was enough to make wrong turn right, it wasn't an excuse. I went around and around in my head trying to justify us both. In the end I wanted to believe him, and not them, tune out my own doubtfulness. *You believe them?* No, son. Goddamn it to hell. Even if my head told me one thing, my heart had a voice all its own — maybe it made no sense to a soul but me, but it sang love. Only song it knew. It was stuck in a groove like a broken old record in its player, couldn't but play the one line, drive everybody to cover their ears. All it knew was that one line, gone what was before or came after, no beginning and no end, just its own music until finally it was heard for what it was, a song in its own right. A love chant powerful because it could never let up, scored deeper until any other music was gone and it grated, hurt to hear and hurt to play.

Cole was smoking on the steps, and when he saw me coming he sprang up and ran into the road, straight into a car and was hit. I saw it all slow, my hand raising up palm flat to show him stop because he was looking back at me, and I saw the car, where it was going and how he couldn't not be hit by it. The car flung him up such a way that he came down on grass, a bed of grass beside the road, saved him from being damaged worse than a fractured collarbone. That night, and a lot of nights after, when I saw my face in the mirror it was bitten with guilt. Seemed to me all the thoughts and worries I had on the inside were pressing their way out, close enough to the surface thin skin only barely kept them hid.

Cole recovered by staying in his room with the door shut, a narrow stripe of light along the bottom all I saw when I passed down the hall. I paused and rested my cheek against the wood doorframe. Maybe he never went to sleep or maybe he left the light on all night. I'd toss fitfully in my bed, in my dreams he was hit by the car, flung up against sky then hard-pulled by gravity — wingless bird, falling angel. I saw Cole's eyes burning black suns.

Was it a sterling accident, or an idea that came to him and he acted on it without thinking to punish me? Did he risk harming himself to punish me for accusing him, calling a spade a spade? Run out and be hit, worth it in his mind to make me suffer. I didn't know how far he would go. How far would I? With Cole I had to prove I loved him by showing him I saw the world out the same window he did. Look at it his way, only his way. See what he wanted me to see. But eyes are wily, vision comes like it or not. They find a way to see even through walls.

I volunteered to take a senior out to lunch once a week, maybe spurred by some of that guilt. I went and picked Mrs. B up at the old age home on Tuesdays, she was always waiting for me just inside the sliding front doors in the lobby, her purse on her lap, her hands shaking the way they did. She was lively, even if frail in her bones. When she saw me she'd nod her head, yes, I'd greet her and she'd keep nodding, yes, yes. "Shoney's," she'd say, and I'd drive us there.

She'd had bad luck with the volunteer before me, who used to pick food off her plate telling her she'd never eat it all anyway, or switch portions if Mrs. B's looked bigger or more appetizing. I let her alone which she seemed thankful for. She'd peruse the menu, then nod yes, yes, and order a hot turkey sandwich. After we ate, she chewed on a plastic toothpick and we drank coffee, hers so loaded thick with sweetener the spoon stood straight up in it.

She liked to talk about her son the astronaut who was down in Florida training to fly to the moon in a rocket ship. Every so often she had her picture made to send him, since he didn't have time to visit her in person anymore. He sent her pictures too, and now that his girlfriend managed a photo store, there was no end to the creative places they could think to put his face. Mrs. B drank her beverages out of a mug with his picture sealed on it, she had a wall calendar with him striking different expressions from month to month, a toothbrush with him on the handle, and a nightgown with his head blazoned life-size on the flannel.

"I don't let myself think it's peculiar," she told me, chewing her toothpick. "But you know, I've forgotten what he looks like with a body and legs. To me my son is just a smiling head. I can't picture him walking on the moon. Rolling on it, maybe. I suppose there are worse things than having a head for a son. Most all the parts of a man I ever had much feeling for were above the neck, anyhow."

It was a long time before I told her I had a son. I told her about Cole, the tornado, the swampy green sky that morning, the flashes of lightning that came one after another like they would never stop and how I went into labor then, destruction all around me.

"Buildings exploded from the inside out," I told her.

"That is the only way to explode, child."

She asked me questions and I talked more, as the weeks went by it getting easier. I had never talked to anyone about Cole, except Ellen maybe and then rarely.

I told her, said out loud, "It's not how I thought it would be."

"You mean he's not." She put her trembling, spotted hand over mine. Though it didn't steady my own shaking, I bent and kissed the darkened marks of age, grateful.

She listened well to me and I spoke to her with relief. The mothers standing on my doorstep blaming me for what Cole did, I told her as best I could, what I saw in their eyes. I closed the door, shut myself in my house.

"It can be hard to tell," she said, "whether a bird is crying or singing. The sounds are so close. The voice comes partly from its genes, partly from experience, and by blending the two it learns to sing. Sometimes birds look so alike, the only way to tell them apart is to hear them sing."

Often Mrs. B fell asleep in the car as I drove back to the seniors' residence, her chin on her chest. I knew about birds — their song evolved from a simple cry aimed at getting attention. They had to cry before they could sing.

After I dropped her off, I used to go to the library and get my books for the week then linger to read. I liked the quiet there, different from the quiet I had at home. The company of strangers, everybody lost in their reading, separate but joined in tranquillity. Books about plants mostly were what I settled down with, but any kind of book to do with nature appealed to me. Not often anymore did I read stories that someone had made up in their imagination. Plants and stars and birds, the moods of weather, were enough for me. I didn't need to have the dazzling bouquet of the human heart laid bare in fiction, to me it was all in the glory of nature.

Sometimes I took my books out to the tumbled-down gazebo in the park beside the library and did my reading under its beadboard roof. The gazebo was octagonal, trimmed in white gingerbread, the paint curled and peeling off in strips, ringed by a moat of perennial blooms. Many of those times, I noticed a man with long shaggy hair in a wheelchair parked in the grass, since no ramp went up to the gazebo's deck. He always had mounds of books piled on his lap, and those days, he was there before I was, still put when I left. I bet he was a Vietnam veteran judging by his age and how he wore his hair so long, as though he was trying to fix himself back before the war when he had a ponytail and his legs took him walking, dancing forever in strawberry fields. I'd read my book, let my eyes drift from the page to him. The sun beat down on him sitting there, and even from where I was, I could see the sweat glistening off him. It was shady where I was.

I went and put the hat right on his head. A big old straw gardening hat of mine with a wide brim, told him, "You ought to keep this on you or be a target for sun cancer."

I'd brought the hat with me one day especially to give him, since it didn't seem he was going to do anything but let himself blister and peel under the sun like the weathered paint on the gazebo. I got to know him after that. I wheeled him under the pecan tree, brought us egg salad sandwiches with tangy mustard pickles, cans of iced tea. His name was Harlin Dade, a friend of mine.

It was his wife got him onto reading after he came back from Vietnam injured in his body, and his mind, with a case of nerves made it he couldn't hold down a real job for long. Every week she'd dump books on him on all kinds of different subjects. Biographies, history books, travel stories, books of philosophy, mysteries, and Harlin would read them. Then if there was something, a certain topic that caught his interest, she'd get him more on it until he was an expert on those subjects. She just kept bringing him books. He traveled to every far-flung country in the world — all inside his head — could tell you what it looked like there, what was special about it. He met a thousand people, or more, he wouldn't feel a stranger with if he met them face to face, because he'd read about their lives. Sitting in the park in the sunshine, Harlin journeyed limitless.

Then his wife told him she was going to see about getting work in a nearby town she'd heard would pay better than where she was now. When she came back she told him she had a job starting Monday, only it was long hours, night shifts. She'd have to move there since it didn't make sense to drive back and forth in the dark. She would stay in the other town Monday to Friday, come home weekends to be with him. She went off and was gone through the week, the weekend Friday to Monday, then the next week of days and the weekend, until Harlin understood he wouldn't be seeing her again. She gave him the world of books, though.

I brought Harlin jonquils and he read to me under the tree. We talked about all kinds of things, including Cole. Between Harlin and Mrs. B, I felt less alone than I had in a long time. The more I talked to them, heard my own voice in my ears, the more I thought somewhere in it I could hear the first tremor of song. Before then I'd had my church mainly for comfort and for fellowship. Until about the time those women came up on the steps accusing Cole of leading their sons astray, the church was my well of strength.

The preacher had us turn around in the pews, shake hands with our neighbors, and when we did, I always looked them in the eye. I might have held their hands too long, I probably did. I think I was trying to tell them something, or I was asking them something, pressing into their palm a sense of what it was like to be me. Or maybe I just wanted to hold somebody's hand that bad.

A Sunday morning Cole got up when I did and asked if he could ride along with me. There was a lake in walking reach of the church — it had been rebuilt after the tornado and its location improved — he planned to take his rod and fish. He thought he could catch a ride, fish while the service was on, then meet up and we'd ride home together after. I should have wondered why he wanted to fish when he could have cared less before.

I never missed a Sunday. The Jesus I knew was kind. He was forgiving of sin. If you admitted what you did wrong, you'd be forgiven. He'd wash your sins away, make you clean. But you had to be truthful about yourself, not prideful or boasting. The sermons preached salvation. Hell and damnation were a last resort. With Jesus in your heart, you could live in the light, though darkness was all around you. You'd be lit from inside.

Sometimes I felt something powerful went on in the church. It started with the singing, built through the preaching, and released with the altar call when people wept and were saved. Found peace. It stayed with me for a while after, personal, fortifying.

From the first week Cole rode with me, there was a strange reaction when church ended and we came out into the parking lot. Members of the congregation got troubled expressions, they wandered puzzled, seeming to have lost where they'd parked their cars. They could swear the cars had been moved, a subtle shift in recall that was waved off. The next week, the same thing. Cars shuffled around as when the tornado had hit, lifted them up, and landed them down someplace else.

Except this time there was Cole, leaning against a tree with his fishing pole, smoking a cigarette even while his lips were twisted at the joke of watching everybody scratch their heads, wander in a fog, thinking was it them, or didn't their cars jump around while they were singing hallelujah?

It didn't make me a genius to figure out Cole had snuck into the cloakroom, rifled through coat pockets for car keys and done himself some test-driving while church was on. Not that he couldn't remember where to park the cars back either, he just didn't want to, wanted to rattle everybody. I thought of poor old Jesus looking down, listening to our nice hymn-

singing with one ear, and to Cole tearing up the roads, dirt flying, radio blasting, with the other ear.

"Get that smirk off your face." We were in the car driving
home. Cole had his feet up on the dash, his elbow out the
window.

"What's your problem?" he said.

"I know. You took those cars."

"Me? Naw, I was fishing."

"Where's the fish?"

He smiled. I looked from him back to the road ahead,
swerved to miss a snake coiled, sunning itself. "Don't lie to me.
You took those cars."

"I didn't take any cars," he said, tuning the radio dial to rock.
"I might have taken them for a ride."

I shook my head. "You think you're so smart. What if you'd
wrecked one of them?"

He shrugged.

"I don't know what to do with you."

"Can't do anything. You're not the boss of me."

"No, well who is?"

"I'm the boss."

"Get out." I pulled over to the side of the road. "I don't want
you in my car."

He sat there looking at the door handle but not putting his
hand on it.

"I mean it," I said. "Get out."

"Come on."

"I'll throw you out myself."

"Try it," he said. But he tugged on the handle, slammed the
door closed behind him.

I drove away. I left him there in a cloud of dust. I thought
back to when he was five and I went and took him from Ellen's.

It was barely dawn and I got him back, my own little boy sitting on the seat beside me. We drove away like we were flying, sky high, it didn't matter then that the clouds were made of dirt. I looked in the rearview, saw Cole walking, small again. I almost turned around and went back for him. But I drove on, it wasn't so far he couldn't walk it, the road led home.

I don't know anyone at church ever cottoned on it was Cole, joyriding while they were saying their prayers. But I didn't want them to know, or him to be charged with theft, or it go on until he was in a wreck. That was it for me. I took to praying in my head and never went back. I watched Oral Roberts on TV and sometimes I felt the spirit move me. I'd put my palms on the screen, feel the energy. But I missed the fellowship. The women in dresses they'd sewn themselves, men in their best shirts didn't have their names stitched over the pockets, missed shaking their hands. I did miss my church, but I just had to leave it all behind.

When that tornado struck and Cole was born out of it, I couldn't have guessed it would come back for him. I tried to keep my feet planted solid and hold onto him as he was pulled from my grip, pulled so hard I could feel myself losing ground. That tornado came back and sucked him into its raging funnel, black as night, and bent on doing damage. I just had to hold on, cleave Cole to me as best I could, for as long as I could.

TWELVE

Cole kept his promise and quit school at sixteen, he wouldn't ever graduate, moved out to a dingy apartment over an army surplus store. He had a roommate named Jess Porter, a tall good-looking boy, like Cole was. They could have both had the world at their feet if they didn't squander their potential, just throw it down the drain. Despite he was moved out on his own, Cole and Jess were at the house a lot off and on, seemed the living room was always a party of teenagers.

I couldn't hardly see them through the haze of pot smoke, bodies on the sofa and sprawled on the floor. I could hear them because they yelled over the music and the clank of beer cans, voices sliding on the edge of a razor, chancy and thin. Mostly they sat in the dark, and if I tried to make it brighter for them, somebody cut the light off again fast. Sometimes things got rowdy and Cole would kick everybody outside where they'd lay around, passed out on the lawn, in front of the neighborhood. By then, none of the neighbors expected better from my house, they'd seen police cars pulled up outside, lights flashing. At first I told myself that at least I knew where Cole was, he was safe, better he did what he was going to do here than anywhere else. But I couldn't pretend I wasn't upset.

Ashtrays overflowing, burn holes in the rug, stink of beer. I told Cole, "This is my house. You need to show respect for it."

"Are you telling me I'm not welcome?" He slurred his words.

"I'm telling you this is my ashtray, this is my rug. It's my house. I don't like you drinking at your age."

"I'm your son," he said. "What's more important to you, me or an ashtray?"

I shook my head. "You and your friends can be here, just you need to be respectful. This is where I live."

"You couldn't wait to get me out, could you, Mama? Live on your own. Too bad you can't give me away again."

"Cole, you don't know."

He flung the ashtray at the wall beside my head. "I'm going," he said.

I took an empty beer can and threw it across the room, but he had already gone.

I hung framed pictures to hide the fight scars on the walls, places Cole had punched his fist through, where pictures wouldn't normally be. My house got quiet.

For long stretches, Cole became a stranger, I didn't know what was going on in his life. I kept hoping it was a stage he'd outgrow, hard teenage years. I didn't let myself add anything up, put it together. Without him, my life was calm, but expectant, I felt like I was waiting for the storm. How to explain the mix of longing and dread? I wouldn't hear anything then I'd get a call to come to the police station. One time they suspected Cole had tried to derail a train by putting concrete blocks on the tracks. They didn't have enough evidence to charge him, but they advised me to leave him locked up overnight, give Cole a taste of a jail cell. For his own good. But that wasn't a taste I wanted him to have, and I brought him out home with me. They told me then it was a mistake, he'd be back, sooner than later. It was just words. Cole said he didn't go near the train tracks, and that was just words too. Seemed everything I heard was *he did this* and *I did not*.

Cole came home with me that time, but there were others I went to the police station to get him and as soon as we were out the doors he went his own way. I'd watch the back of him until he rounded a corner. The waiting I did — some of it was waiting to blend the Cole of my heart, my son, with this tired, scraggy youth in jeans coming out of the police station, carrying his belongings in a paper sack, pushing the money I'd given him into his pocket while he walked away from me.

Cole moved around, still coming back to my house to live, and party, if he was between places. His old roommate Jess coasted with him, was in and out of trouble too, but he had a softer side, most of the trouble he caused was for himself. Jess couldn't keep a job, or keep from being stoned. He played the guitar with a slide on his finger, pulled songs from the strings that haunt me to this day. Cole and his friends would be in the living room, asleep or drunk or stoned, and Jess would take up the guitar. I swear it called to me, and I had to come stand in the doorway. I felt those notes strum something in me, low and true. I watched Jess hunched over the guitar in his lap, his fingers pressing and moving on it, making it ache under his touch so it had to do what he wanted, surrender to him.

He'd glance up from the guitar and see me, a look of dazed bliss in his eyes. I thought the music was a room we could meet in. A place outside of this house and this world. There weren't walls. We were in it together, he heard what I heard, and I wasn't alone. That music, I thought, was the sound of Jess. It tore a piece out of him to play — was its beauty — that it cost him.

He could have gone anywhere, just a kid, but he was going nowhere. I didn't like to think he wouldn't try to make something of himself. I thought about his music, if it sprang from hope or despair, the thin line between. A bird crying or learning to sing? One night Jess came into my bedroom, stood lingering shiftless in the dark so that it woke me up. He got down on his knees beside the bed and looked at me.

"Jess?" I said.

Tears streamed down his face.

"What is it?" I put my hand to his cheek. He cried, looking at me the whole time, scared rabbits in his eyes. I stroked the back of his head, his hair soft and thick. "What's wrong, Jess?" I folded back the covers and moved so he could climb into the bed beside me. I held him in my arms.

"Whatever it is," I spoke barely a whisper, "it'll pass." Like Cole, he was on that rocky ledge between being a boy and a man. He was on the edge of something else, too, more treacherous. He knew it. To get from where he was, he'd have to climb a mountain of ice. He could do it, but the easier way was slide down.

I felt the wet of his tears dampening my nightdress. He pressed close against me. "It'll be okay," I said. "Get to sleep." I hummed some of the song he'd played earlier that I could still hear in my head. He shifted and I felt him stir against my hip and grow hard. He pushed the stiffness against me, maybe a natural impulse of his body. "Jess," I said. His chest was smooth in the moonlight, his skin the color of honey. He pushed again and I closed my eyes. For an instant I let the walls fall away, and we were in that room again, outside time and space. Only the thrumming guitar, slide of his finger, long pull of the notes, a low chord being held. He tried to turn me to him. "No," I said. I was shamed my body had responded, even if he didn't know it had. Not long after, his breathing went deep and I laid awake beside him. He was gone in the morning, gone for months.

Routinely twenty dollars went missing from my purse, more if I had it. Just as the money went missing, so did Cole. I'd confronted him about it before, but it didn't do any good, I slept with my car keys and wallet under my pillow.

Harlin suffered a bout of nerves and was confined recuperating at the veterans hospital. Everybody except Mrs. B disappeared from me at times. It was as if the sound was muted on a loud television program, and all sudden you heard yourself breathing, the house shifting, creaking in the dark, settling in its earth bed. I watched my garden flowers blossom and fade, a cycle of deadheading the old to let the new take the light, draw nurture. Butterflies basked on the petal ledges, cold-blooded, though so beautiful. They slept by themselves at night. To fly they needed the heat of the sun.

I'd visit Harlin now and then at the hospital, toting a simple arrangement for him all of a color, maybe lacy whites, or purples, yellow wildflowers. But sometimes they'd given him so many drugs he couldn't wake up to see me, or else he'd just gaze away out the window, or at the ceiling, and I didn't know if he knew who I was. His friend.

"Harlin, I brought you flowers," I'd tell him, "and they're all blue." He might keep his eyes closed, even if he heard me. Maybe the light was too strong, it hurt his eyes. Maybe he was tired of seeing anything. I'd pull a chair beside his bed, keep my voice hushed.

I read out loud from books to him. I told him about the Canadian north where I spent my summers. Thousands of years ago it was covered by a gigantic sheet of ice two miles thick, frozen solid all year long. Then the world heated up and the ice melted into scatters of clear lakes. "I swam in those lakes, and clear as they were, they had secrets. Deep down, they kept their treasures to themselves." I told him lines in the bedrock show which way the ice flowed so long ago. By the shore, the rocks are granite, pink as the sky blushing at the morning's kiss. "Harlin, hear me? The rocks are pink."

It was like talking to myself. I'd set the flowers I brought him on the windowsill. "I hope you like them. They're fragrant, and did I tell you they're blue?" I'd lean my arms on his bed.

"I saw a rosebush once, Harlin, when I was a child, and all the roses on it were blue. It made my mama cry. But I thought it was pretty. Blue roses. I still dream about it, only in my dream, Mama doesn't cry. We're putting sweetheart roses on a little grave. The grave of my drowned puppy, and Ellen is holding my hand. When she smiles at me, her mouth is full of blue petals."

"I have to believe, Harlin, a person learns from their mistakes."

"Do you think it's ever too late to change, Harlin?"

"Does love mean anything but saying you're sorry?"

When he was nearly all recovered, he was allowed out of the hospital for day-long excursions and I invited him for an early supper. Harlin hadn't been to my house before, and I wanted to make sure it looked tidy and clean for him as a first, lasting impression. I went out of my way to get a good cut of beef from the butcher and dark coffee beans ground fresh from the Moonbean Cafe, which made the best coffee.

I baked a big dish of scalloped potatoes, and buttermilk biscuits. I was bending to check the roast in the oven, wearing but my slip, when Cole and five of his friends walked in the door behind me. I hadn't seen my son in months. His arm was trussed in a sling and he had a black eye. I already had the dining table set with wine glasses and folded napkins. The glasses were good crystal of Mama's that I'd washed in extra hot soapy water and dried to a sparkle.

Cole said, "What's going on?"

"I'm having company. A dinner guest."

"Who?"

"You don't know him. His name's Harlin," I said. "My friend Harlin Dade."

"A man?" Cole picked one of the cloth napkins off the table so the pleats I'd carefully made fell out, dropped it down again along with a shock of ash from his cigarette. "You got a date, Mama?"

"No, I told you. He's my friend."

"I hope you're going to wear more than that."

I saw they were all looking at me in my slip. Jess, two girls, and two boys I hadn't ever seen.

"You better," Cole said. "Take those rollers out while you're at it." My hand went to my hair, the other arm across the thin silk covering my chest.

Cole walked into the living room and they followed him, carrying six-packs.

"Cole? Can I talk to you?" I called, and he hung back.

He came into the kitchen. I said, "My friend, he's — he—"

"Spit it out."

"He has a condition."

"Oh yeah?"

"He was in the war. In Vietnam," I said. "So now —"

"What is he, crazy?"

"No, he's not crazy."

"You have a date with a crazy man, Mama?"

"He's not. But he's been in the hospital, he's still recovering. He's out on a pass."

Cole pressed the bruise under his eye with his finger. He looked blank, I couldn't tell if it hurt to touch or not.

"I don't want you to bother him. Okay?"

"Bother him?" Cole said.

"I don't want you to make too much noise. I need it to be peaceful."

Cole's look turned bitter. The blackened eye was blood-shot. He turned his head with disdain, spoke to the wall. "It's good to see you too, Mama. Thanks for asking what happened to me."

"I wondered what happened, Cole. Were you in a fight?"

"Naw, Mama." He shifted his weight, lifted his chin. "I didn't get no chance to fight back." He strode then into the living room, and I heard him tell his friends, "Looks like we're in time for dinner. My mama's got a date." A can of beer opened with a hiss. "A date with a crazy man."

It was too late to call Harlin now and tell him not to come. A wheelchair bus had been arranged to transport him back and forth from the hospital, would give us just enough time to have dinner and talk. I couldn't call him now. I didn't know how to guess what Cole would do, how he'd act. The dining room connected to the living room in an L shape with no doors in between, I saw Jess with his shoes on the coffee table, his arm anchored around one of the girls, lips locked on her neck, branding a hickey on her maybe. Cole's back was to me, look-ing through a stack of music tapes. I felt like I was on a roller-coaster, clanking slow up the rise, too late to get off. I shook the fallen ash from the napkin, pleated it back how it was. I touched the stem of a wine glass, the crystal shone fine.

I went into my bedroom to get dressed, stared into the closet. It wasn't a date with Harlin. It wasn't, but somehow I'd come to love him so much as a friend, I wanted everything to be perfect for him. I wanted to please him. I pulled out a dress, the same buttercup yellow as the first sleeper I bought for Cole even before he was born. The dress had a low neckline, tight waist, long skirt. I still had a nice figure it showed off. That was the only thing of mine Ellen ever wanted for herself. Sometimes when we were teenagers, she came in when I was taking a bath. She'd look at my body in the water, my breasts, and tell me I was lucky to be cut like Mama, instead of getting our daddy's big bones like she did. I knew she thought it was unfair, my body should have been hers.

It was a crush I had on Harlin. It didn't seem right when all he'd ever been to me was my friend, but the truth was, sometimes I imagined kissing him tenderly, kissing his mouth. I wondered what he'd be able to do in bed. I couldn't help myself. I'd crossed a line. Attraction made sense fly out the window. Lust came in on the breeze, riding bareback on the air.

I heard voices from the living room getting louder. I took the rollers out of my hair, combed it, my hand shaking. I put on mascara and lipstick. My cheeks were flushed on their own.

I hadn't given a thought to how we would get the wheelchair up the steps into the house. When the time came, the bus driver deposited Harlin on the walk and sped off after ringing the bell. Unless there was a ramp in place, that's where his duty ended. Harlin had put on a suede vest with a fringe, and tied his hair back in a ponytail. He said, "Whoa, baby," when he saw me. I tried to smile. He seemed the same as always, except for an eyelid twitch that must have come on lately with the nerves.

I told him, "My son and his friends are here. They showed up just a while ago." I sighed. "I don't think they'll bother us. Please come in. Let me help you." He rolled his wheelchair to the bottom of the stairs and turned it backwards.

"It's heavy, Grace. Maybe you could get Cole to come out. You have to pull the chair up a step at a time, it takes some hauling."

"Cole's got a broken arm," I said. "But wait here."

I went inside. The living room was smoky and music was playing, the curtains were drawn. Jess was on the couch with his head flung back, eyes closed, his girlfriend's feet in his lap. I couldn't tell if he was asleep, or stoned, or listening to the music. Cole and some others were by turns flipping coins into a glass, banging on the table, a drinking game. "Excuse me," I said.

Everybody held what they were doing and stared at me. Cole turned. "Is dinner ready?"

"I was wondering if someone could help me with my guest?" I was looking at Jess, who'd raised his head to stare at me with all the other pairs of eyes. "Jess, could you help me? Cole can't with his arm broken."

"Do what?" Jess was pushing his girlfriend's feet off him, her fighting to keep them there.

"Should we sit at the table, Mama?" Cole said. "It smells good."

"I'm having company for dinner, Cole. You know I wasn't expecting you."

"Don't you want us on your date?" He hit the last word.

"I'll save you some food for after we're done. Jess, are you going to help me?"

He got up from the couch like he had to break its suction first.

"Where's your boyfriend, Mama?" Cole said, his back already to me.

Jess came outside and when he saw Harlin in the wheelchair he raised his eyebrows, but he didn't say anything.

"Harlin, this is Jess Porter. He's a friend of my son's."

"Jess," Harlin said, and held out his hand, and thankfully Jess shook it. Harlin told him what to do.

I went up the steps ahead of them to hold open the door.

Cole was standing just inside watching. "Can you get the door?"
I said to him.

"Naw, I can't," he said, backing away. Then when I got closer,
he leaned into my ear, "Too bad your boyfriend's a cripple."

I pushed him aside and he kept going on back to the living
room. Jess got Harlin into the house and no further.

"I can take it from here," Harlin said. "I appreciate your
help."

I showed Harlin to the dining table, had him park with his
back to where Cole and his friends were, facing the wallpaper
and me only. I brought out the wine and our dinner, served us
right away. I could hardly eat. Every clatter from the living
room was like glass in my blood. I kept checking over Harlin's
shoulder, make sure no trouble was coming our way. I poured
the wine, drank it faster every time. I couldn't concentrate on
what he was saying. More and more wine. I thought I heard
Cole's voice calling me, above the music, noise of his friends.

"Did you want something, son?" I called back. It hung in
the air, got no answer.

"Relax," Harlin said to me.

I nodded. I raised my glass.

"Cheers," he said, and he took a sip.

And after a while I did relax. I let Harlin be all I saw. I
admired every line on his face for its own sake, the deep bands
around his mouth, his crow's-feet. I didn't let myself hear anything but the flow of his words, warm waves over me. I thought
of leaning forward and kissing his mouth. I wanted to. Taste the
wine on his lips. I wanted to put my hands on him, any way I
could to connect with him, like I used to when Cole was small
and not mine, and I'd visit him at Ellen's, it was the same longing for touch. Only this was something else, too — I wanted
to kiss Harlin hard.

He had stopped talking and was looking at me straight on. He'd caught me, read my daydream, seen it clearly as though it was flashing on my forehead, instead of private in my mind. My hand flew up and covered my mouth, as if that would stop him from saying anything, telling me to give it up. "I'm sorry," I said through my fingers. "Forgive me."

He checked his watch and I thought he had a slight smile. "Dessert?" he said.

I was already standing to run to the kitchen, take a wait and collect myself. There, I turned on the water taps full to drown out my chastising myself. What was the matter with me? I held onto the counter to keep the room from spinning me off balance. I loved my friend. That wasn't right, I knew it. I desired him. My cheeks were burning. I listened to the water rushing like Niagara Falls. I thought of Jackson and wanted to cry. All that water pouring down the drain.

Then I calmed myself with the thought I hadn't done any-thing. Maybe it was all in my head, private where it belonged. Nothing wrong had happened. It was the wine, made anything seem possible. Thinking wasn't doing, Harlin couldn't guess the inner workings of my brain. I felt more composed. I hadn't done anything. I got on with fixing our dessert, but I could smell myself as I walked around the kitchen, the ripeness of myself down there, all that want. Then I just didn't know what to think.

When I came out of the kitchen, Harlin was in the living room with Cole and his friends. He was taking a hash pipe out of his vest pocket. I put the cake plate down on the dining table, sat and cut myself a slice. I watched as he filled the pipe with hash and Cole lit it, passed it around. They were all lean-ing in, a closed circle. The smoke from the pipe filled the room and drifted over to where I was. My head was swimming.

Somebody laughed and I wondered if it could be Cole. I could but eat my cake, drink my wine.

Then the bus was back for him. Without me having to ask, Jess and another boy carried Harlin in his wheelchair down the stairs, kept him so steady upright he could have been sitting on a throne.

I gave Harlin a wedge of cake wrapped in foil for later. He looked at me serenely with glistening eyes, big black hoops, all pupil. I noticed the twitch was gone from his eyelid. "You honor me, Grace."

He was one of those people who don't look away, they look and look at you until you know they must be seeing what you are, not what you're holding up to show. It takes getting used to.

He wheeled onto the elevator platform that would raise him into the bus. As he was lifting up, I blew him a kiss. I would let the air decide whether it found his lips.

When I turned around, Cole and his friends were leaving the house, had their jackets on. "I can get you some dinner now," I said.

"Forget it." Cole was lighting a cigarette, shook out the match.

"Jess, are you hungry? Thank you for helping me." I nodded at the other boy who'd also helped.

Jess waved, following Cole. The two girls were walking ahead of them.

"Are you coming back?" I called.

Jess and Cole looked at each other. "Naw," Cole said. "Not for a while."

"Bye," I said.

I sat on the front steps for what seemed like a long time, my head pounding. Then I went inside and ran myself a hot bath. I laid back in the water, just me again. I thought about Cole, and Harlin, and Jackson. Each their own particular torture to me, their own pleasure. My loves. I thought about Jackson carrying bodies out of burning buildings while they still had life in them. The life in a body felt by a pulse in the neck or wrist. But I wondered if life wasn't felt somewhere more remote, more secret, as want. The want I felt for Harlin at dinner, so strong I breathed it in the air like oxygen.

Later that night, a noise woke me up when I was sleeping in bed. I raised my head off the pillow so I could hear better, waited listening. I strained to hear and it seemed the sound of nothing was even a sound in my ears. Then I heard a shard of a deep voice, brittle in the night.

"Cole?" I called, and I regretted it.

I didn't know if I should have kept quiet, pulled the blankets up around me and pretended I was asleep. I thought briefly maybe I hadn't heard anything. But then another noise and I had to get up and see who was in my living room.

Walking down the hallway with no windows, the ground was pitch black under my feet, and I took slow steps. Probably it was Cole and his friends back again, but they didn't usually try to hush or be considerate when they came in. Then there was a loud crash from the china cabinet, the sound of my mama's crystal glasses breaking. After, nothing again, thick dull silence in the dark. I felt like I was under water, at the bottom of a black lake. The smash of glass still in my ears, only in my head.

I flicked on the light in the living room. Two boys wearing sweatshirts with hoods were carrying my television between them. The door to the china cabinet was open, glass all over the floor.

"Cole?" I said. The one boy looked to be about the same height and size as Cole. "What are you doing?"

"Come on," the other one said.

I went and pulled the hood off so I could see my son's face. But it wasn't. In an instant, with a mix of relief then fear, I saw it was the boy who'd helped Jess carry Harlin down the steps like he was a king.

"Fuck," he said, and they dropped the TV. He had my hair bunched in his hand before I could move, wrenched it hard until I was on my knees on the ground.

"Let's go," the other boy said.

"She seen me." He jerked my hair with every word, so I cried out and clawed at his fingers, trying to pry them off. "You're going to be sorry now," he told me.

His fist exploded into my cheek, white ice, shattering everything in my head. The ceiling spun, from flat on the floor the furniture legs were crazy angled, unreal. Far off I heard an awful whimpering, and when I got raspy in my throat, I understood it was me. I was crawling somewhere. Where did I think I was going?

He held me down with one hand tightening on my neck to stop me from screaming, used the other to punch. Only sound now his heavy breathing. Only his because I'd given it up. I dimly wondered how long could it go on? It was remarkable, pound, pound, pound. I was nothing. My tongue was so swollen huge in my mouth I thought I would choke on it. I was suffocating. It wasn't white anymore but black.

The first thought that came to me after was his words telling me I was going to be sorry now. Now. But I was already sorry then. Because I loved Cole, it meant I was. From the day of his birth when I looked at him through the glass wall, and could just stand watch. Love wasn't enough and sorry wasn't enough, he was on his own. For a long time I laid there, didn't think I could open my eyes, tears still running out the sides of them down my temples into my hair.

The first face I saw was a police officer's crouched over me, then Cole standing above him. Cole's face was wet, big tears of his own. I blinked, pain shot through my skull. I tried to open my mouth but I couldn't feel where it was.

Cole and Jess had come back to the house while the other boys were still looting the silverware, and some of my mama's jewelry that was worth nothing except to me. Cole saw the TV off its stand, the smashed crystal, my body on the floor as dead. A fight broke out between them, Cole with his arm broken in a sling. A knife got pulled. The one boy held Cole's good arm behind his back, so the other could come at him with the knife. By accident or not, Jess stepped in front. He took the blade in his lung. The robbers fled out the kitchen door. Jess died with his head cradled in Cole's arm. He slipped through Cole's fingers like water. An ocean of tears.

Nothing was the same after that. Jess was buried in an old cemetery beside his maternal grandfather, in the deep shade of an oak tree with branches that flowed down to the graves. As Jess was being lowered into the earth, his mother threw herself on top of his casket. Cole and the preacher each together pulled her out. All around, old stone crosses and headstones stood every which way in the ground, some shoved up from below, others sunk in almost entirely, the names, dates of birth and death, lost underground. Brick vaults were heaved up in the grass cracked and crumbling, as though the dead below had found no peace, were restless.

Sleeping pills got me through the nights while I healed slow as molasses, let me not hear every creak or owl in the trees outside my window. I was left with a bad scar where my lip had split in such a way it was hard for them to stitch it neatly in place. The line of my lip was jagged. When I went to smile, I felt it pull, a part couldn't be brought up even with the rest. It held back.

Cole almost never came to the house then. He didn't want to look at me, think of Jess. He got a job with a traveling fair that took him from county to county. He was a stunt rider, rode a motorcycle at an attraction called The Wall of Death. It was a round wooden structure, like a steep donut, with stairs going up the outside. People would climb to the top and gather around looking down into the middle. The inner walls were wood and the motorcycles would come in through a trap door at the bottom that was then latched closed before the show started. Sometimes they rode one at a time, or else, dangerously, two bikes would ride in tandem not more than a few inches apart.

They'd get on the bikes, rev the engines, deafeningly loud, powerful, throbbing motors so the whole structure vibrated, felt flimsy. Children covered their ears with their hands. Then the riders would climb the motorcycles up the walls, circling around faster and faster defying gravity, horizontal to the ground, so if it wasn't for the speed they would fall. Buzzing like a million angry hornets in a bucket, higher and higher, until they were zigging impossibly around the very top edge, the floor alive under people's feet. They'd play chicken with the crowd then, darting the bikes almost too close towards them, almost. Everybody jumped back, thrilled. They played chicken with each other too, vying for the lead by turns racing in front, nearly clipping tires. So fast they were a blur.

The last stunt they did, after standing up on the bikes, driving side by side with arms linked, was to ask the audience members, those who dared, to put their wrists over the top ledge and hold a quarter out between their fingers for the daredevil rider to collect. Cole did the act alone, while the other rider waited on the ground. Cole took the money at lightning speed, so expertly that people didn't know without checking it was gone. He hardly ever dropped a coin.

When the show was over, Cole shifted gears gyrating down the walls, cut the engine, and took a showman's bow at the bottom. Then they thanked everyone for coming and told them how their lives were risked at every performance, and since the death-defying nature of the stunts meant they couldn't get insurance coverage, maybe the audience could show their appreciation. Coins rained from above like a summer downpour. Bills fluttered to their feet like autumn leaves. The riders got a broom and swept up the money. There was only a ten-minute break between shows for them to stand out back, smoke a cigarette, and wipe away the sweat. Maybe it was while Cole was whirling in the vortex at top speed, a roaring wind snatching money from people, he thought to save himself the trouble, get a gun.

BUTTERFLIES

Butterflies don't see clearly. Their huge compound eyes are made up of many facets, or simple eyes, causing the butterfly to see everything as a mass of tiny pictures. While each precise image may be clear, when put together as a whole, the combined big picture is less than sharp. Yet butterflies can see what is invisible to man; they can see ultraviolet light. Photographs taken on special film have shown that many flowers and butterflies are decorated with ultraviolet designs. Hidden is a secret world of vibrant beauty.

THIRTEEN

Cole had a way with Ivy, he'd treat her mean as a hornet, dampen her spirit down, then come loving up on her. I called him at the motel, told him I'd found them a small furnished apartment that could be rented month to month. It was nothing fancy, a red-brick building, one bedroom flat at the top of two narrow flights of stairs. It had a fair-sized kitchen with a table and chairs, a boxy living room, an old bathroom with a clawfoot tub, no shower. The only window was in the bedroom and faced the back of another building across an alley, and the garbage dumpster. I thought it would be private and close enough to the center of the town that if they took jobs they'd be able to walk to work.

"You're going to have to come get us. We'll be ready," Cole said.

I heard Ivy in the background saying something muffled by distance, and all the phone lines and wires.

"I'll stop and pick you up some supplies, groceries, on my way. Anything you want especially? I've got your clothes packed."

"Naw, whatever. Cigarettes."

"Does Ivy want something?"

"No."

"You want to ask her?"

"She don't need anything, Mama."

I heard Ivy again. Heard her clearly, closer to the phone. She said, "Why can't I go out? Nobody's looking for me."

"Just come get us," Cole said.

"I need some goddamn tampons," Ivy shouted.

There was a pause. "You hear that?" Cole said.

"Tampons, uh huh." I don't think I'd ever said that word out loud before. "Anything else?"

"No."

"Sure?"

I heard from Ivy, "Hand me the phone . . . Grace? Can you get some cinnamon and some sugar for hot cinnamon toast?" She covered the phone, but I heard her tell Cole to shut up and let go. I guessed he was trying to wrench the phone off her. "It's my bedtime snack, okay? So what's wrong with that?" There was a scuffle then.

"That all, Ivy?" I said. "Hello? Cole?" It sounded like the phone was kicked flying then I heard Ivy laugh just before it got hung up. I thought she was laughing. Maybe they were stir-crazy, holed up in the motel.

I thought of my son kissing his wife, taking the woman he'd married in his arms and falling onto the bed, smiles on their lips. Man and wife falling down together. If you could find a person to lay with in the world, so you didn't wake up at dawn the sheets cold beside you, you were lucky. I'd loved Cole the whole of his life, but I couldn't keep him out of trouble, maybe Ivy could now. It was up to her. Cole held something, it snapped in his fingers. Whatever it was, always happened like that. I worried for Ivy she'd be snapped apart in his hands. But she was strong, not so easily damaged. I worried it wasn't her but Cole who'd be split in half, cracked down the middle neatly through his heart. Look where love had brought him so far. On the run from jail. No wonder Ivy wouldn't be wrecked by him, he couldn't quite get hold of her, his wife flitted just beyond his reach.

Driving to the motel, every car I passed or passed me was in my mind a police car. My hands were sweating on the wheel, my eyes darted to the rearview. When I stopped for gas, I kept my head lowered, barely breathing, drove off cautiously, obeying all the rules of the road. As soon as I pulled up at the door to their room, they came out. They must have been waiting, watching for me through the curtains. They both had sunglasses on and Ivy turned her face up to the sky for a moment. She looked prettier than ever, her midriff bare, high-heeled sandals making her legs look even longer. She stretched slinky as a cat. Cole hadn't shaved, washed, or combed his hair, and despite the dark glasses, he covered his eyes with his hand when the light hit.

On the way to the apartment I told them what it looked like, though they were about to see for themselves, how the location was such they could walk to work if they took jobs in town. Neither of them bothered to comment.

"I noticed there was a garage," I said to Cole. "Maybe you could get work as a mechanic." He knew about cars and motorcycles from stunt riding, and that ability he always had to take things apart and mostly fit them together again. I looked over at him but he was gazing out the side window. "There was a music store too. Well, you'll see. We're almost there." I was talking like nobody was listening, felt mildly despised for scribbling the silence with doodles. I wanted this to be a new start for them, for Cole and Ivy as a couple, but no matter what I said I couldn't escape the notion that it was borrowed time. I knew better than to pretend a pall wasn't over us.

They followed me up the steps and I unlocked the door to the apartment. As soon as we got inside, Cole turned the deadbolt·

and fastened the chainlock. They looked around the rooms, try-ing out the furniture, flushing the toilet, while I went to unpack the groceries in the kitchen. I tried to put things into some kind of order for them in the cupboards. A closet door creaked open in the hall.

"Check this out," Ivy said. "There's a bunch of old movies in here." She read the titles. "*The Crimson Pirate, From Here to Eternity, Come Back Little Sheba, The Rose Tattoo, The Rainmaker, Elmer Gantry, Vera Cruz, Birdman of Alcatraz, Atlantic City*. I saw *Atlantic City*. There must be a dozen videotapes."

"Those all star Burt Lancaster," I said.

"Who?"

"Burt Lancaster. He was a swashbuckler. He did his own stunts."

"Cole likes stunts," she said. "There's a TV and a VCR." It was the happiest I'd heard her. "Baby, we can watch movies."

I didn't hear if Cole answered or not. I'd bought the ingre-dients to make chili for dinner, a big pot so they'd have some left over to reheat another night. I was opening the cans of kid-ney beans and plum tomatoes when Cole put his hand on my shoulder, made me jump out my skin.

"Ivy'll cook," he said. "You go on sit down, Mama."

"I don't mind."

"Ivy?" he called in my ear.

It took a while for her answer to float from the other room. "What?"

"Leave her, son. I'm fine," I said. I pulled a skillet out from beneath the counter and put the ground beef on the burner to brown.

"Naw. Ivy?" he called again. "She can make our dinner. You sit down."

"What!"

"Get in here. Cook us some chili."

"I'm picking a movie."

Cole drew a breath, opened his mouth, but I put my hand up. "She's just in the next room," I said. "Why not go in there and talk to her instead of hollering through the walls."

Cole stood glued for a second, then he strode out of the kitchen. Videos clattered to the floor, harsh words shot back and forth. They were both young and stubborn as mules. I could bet she wouldn't boil water for him now for pride's sake, and he wouldn't let her off the hook for the same reason, he was bent on making her do what he wanted. They were like little kids tugging war, only a short length of rope between them, no slack cut. A yawning pit of mud monkeyed in the middle, both gritting their teeth and pulling the other, heels dug in.

I heard Ivy thundering across the floorboards before I saw her glowering into the pot of beans and tomatoes with her hands on her hips. "You need help, Grace, or what?"

"I don't. I'm fine," I said. "I'm just going to chop an onion, and a green pepper, then throw them in to simmer. That's all."

"She's just going to chop an onion," she told Cole. "She doesn't need my help." She told him even though he was standing there throughout, and didn't need a recap.

"What's the matter with you?" he said to her.

"Only you," she said. "You're the only thing the matter with me."

"Okay," I said. "Now we'll let it simmer for an hour."

"I'm taking a bath," Ivy said, turning on her heels.

We both watched her go, heard the taps come on in the bathroom.

"I don't guess it's easy for her," I said. "She's had to make a life for herself without you, while you were in jail. That's all shaken up now. Don't forget, she's here with you, after all.

What are you going to do next? You have to start over now."

"I've been thinking the only chance for us is to get far from here, maybe Mexico or Canada. I got to get some money for that. The more money, easier everything'll be."

"Are you thinking you might go down to that garage for a job?"

Cole rolled a cigarette, licked the paper closed, lit it, drew deep. The smoke came out with his words like they were balls of fire.

"Naw, I ain't. Face it, Mama, I know how to do a job. You know what I mean? I do jobs."

"You can put the past behind you. It's your choice."

"Nobody's going to clock my ass. Tell me do this, do that. Fuck it. Some Joe sleeping in his bed, his wife beside him, kids down the hall — I break a window quiet, in and out."

"I thought you were done with that. I thought you wanted a clean slate, start fresh."

"That's what you want. You want a clean slate for yourself."

"I do. I want things to change. That's my hope."

"Things'll change. A couple of B-and-Es, maybe an armed robbery, and adios — I'll send you a postcard."

"What about Ivy?"

"She's coming."

"What if Joe wakes up in his bed, takes a gun from under his pillow?"

"Adios, I guess. But no postcard."

"Remember Jess?" I said. I wanted to hurt him. Slap him out of being glib. "Remember what happened to me?" He brought his cigarette up to his mouth, his hand was trembling as he raised it. He was looking at the scar on my lip.

I thought by being his mother, my life was tied to his. Cole was sinking in quicksand. How far in was he — up to his knees, his waist, up to his neck? But I'd go down with him if I trusted my strength alone could pull him out. If I ran to put my arms around him, we'd be lost. But then if I stood back, if I didn't lift a finger, I'd lose him. We were lost too. Maybe if Ivy took his hand, and I took hers, there was a chance together we'd get him free of what was dragging him down.

"This don't have anything to do with you," Cole said. "And Jess is dead." He flicked the butt into the sink.

"Listen. I'm here, damn it. I'm hiding you out. Cooking on your stove. We're all bandits now," I said stupidly, and my voice broke. "I don't know when I'll see you again. If you'll just be gone."

"Mama," he said. "You got to know the cops'll be hounding you. If it isn't already, your phone'll be tapped. They're going to try to make you tell where I am. I got to raise some money. Until then we'll be right here. Okay? You know where we are. We'll get a phone hooked up under a fake name. Then it'll be safe to call us from a pay booth."

"B. Lancaster," I said. "He was a swashbuckler." I turned to stir the chili, swirling it around and around. The drab lighting in the kitchen made everything, the walls, the cupboards, the clock, a yellowy brown like gold that had tarnished. A shiver caught the nape of my neck, an icy finger down my spine. I thought of the ancient glacier that froze the Canadian north. It couldn't be stopped from spreading over the land, burying trees and mountains, pushing them under miles of ice. And I thought of Ivy and me. The prison guard Cole stuck with the metal pipe, the store clerk he hit with the bat, and who else? The weight of tons of ice, so cold blood froze.

I sat at the kitchen table, caught in a web of time, the past catching up to the future. I couldn't look back and I couldn't look ahead either. I was stuck in the present, nowhere to go, nothing to do but wait, dare to hope something would change. I put out the bowls, poured three glasses of milk. I took the pot off the burner. I went to knock on the bathroom door, tell Ivy the dinner was ready, but it wasn't closed. The door was ajar enough I could see Cole was in the bathtub with her. They were sitting facing each other, white suds of shampoo on their heads, Cole massaging Ivy's scalp, up to his wrists in foam. She had her eyes shut but her mouth was moving, telling him something. Again they struck me as little kids. I put the pot back on the burner to simmer some more.

After dinner Cole went into the bedroom, looked out the window behind the bed, was already putting on his jacket when he came into the living room. "It's dark enough," he said. "I'm going out."

He pulled on his basketball runners. The way he was bent down, the arc of his back, the slight curl to his hair, he could have been Jackson. It could have been his father right there, like seeing a ghost.

Ivy was on the floor sorting through the videotapes, and I was drinking a cup of Chinese green tea before I drove home, when Cole said he was leaving.

"I thought we were going to watch a movie," Ivy pouted.

"Later maybe." Cole stood and the specter of Jackson was still inside him. Something made me think that Jackson had stepped in, was protecting him from within, shielding him. A knot tightened in my stomach. A dead man in my boy. It scared me to think maybe nobody on earth could protect him.

"But we had it planned," Ivy said. "There's a VCR."

"You can watch," Cole said. "Who's stopping you?"

"I want to come," she said. "Wait for me."

"I told you. There might be cops. There might be trouble."

"I'm coming."

"You're staying here." He launched his eyes to the ceiling as if there might be a secret exit, a way out faster than he was getting out the door. Then he made an effort to soften his tone. "Mama'll watch with you, won't you?"

"Sure," I said.

Ivy made a face. "I wanted to watch a movie with you. Be with you. Forget it," she said.

"I'll hurry back, okay?"

"Don't bother."

Cole hesitated, looked to me. "I'll catch you later, Mama."

"Alright," I said.

"Thanks," he said.

"Uh huh."

He still stood waffling, and I knew he was thinking what he could say to patch things up with Ivy before he went. I could feel her hanging, waiting to hear it. Something he could say so bad vibes wouldn't be left between them. What could he say? I peered into my teacup to keep myself out of it.

"Lock the door," he said. Then the sound of closing shut, saddest sound in the world. The door closing on an opportunity.

Ivy shuffled the movie boxes forlornly, reading the backs, putting them down. She reminded me of Cole when he had nobody to play with him, only me for company, not his first choice. I did what I used to do then, went into the kitchen to make something sweet.

I brought her a plate with a stack of hot cinnamon toast. She'd picked a movie, *Birdman of Alcatraz*.

"You know that's a true story," I said. "Well, a Hollywood true story."

"No kidding."

"Robert Stroud was in solitary confinement for fifty years."

"What did he do?"

"I think he killed somebody. Another inmate, I think. You know he never did get released. He died in custody, though by then it wasn't maximum-security, it wasn't Alcatraz. They let him off the Rock when he was an old man, a real old man."

"So it's right up our alley," she said and laughed, with no lightness in it. She pushed the video into the slot and the opening credits flashed. "Do they explain why he did it? I like to know why."

"I saw it a long time ago. I guess I don't remember why. Just he was locked up by himself all that time. I remember the cages of birds. They were canaries, but the movie was in black and white. There was no color to the birds, shades of gray. Not a single yellow canary. Why, is the whole movie. You have to see it all to understand him."

Ivy ate the toast then put the plate of crumbs on the floor. I don't know how long after I realized she was asleep.

I don't know if she saw the part where the Birdman tells his wife to give up on him. She fought her heart out for him, but he tells her the sun's gone down, and she shouldn't look for it to rise again. Pretend I'm a dead man. He wants her to pretend she's standing on his grave. He doesn't want her to waste her life on him, throw away her own freedom. They gave him a life sentence and life was what they were going to take. His not hers. She still has a dance or two left, he tells her. The way she cried then, pressed her hand to the glass wall between them, it was hard to imagine her ever wanting to dance. It didn't look like her feet could carry her anywhere, if she even knew where to go.

I took the cover from the bed, laid it over Ivy. She didn't stir and I shut the lights, went out locking the door behind me with the key I had. It was raining when I stepped outside, cool splashes hit my face, and after the closed air of the apartment, it felt fine. A small thing, rain. But when I stood with my head tipped back, mouth open, it tasted like freedom.

In the movie, the Birdman of Alcatraz sends his sparrow out into the world, makes it fly away through the prison bars. But it comes back to be with him. Clear on his face is how happy he is to see it again, that it hurts him too. He holds the little sparrow in his hand up to the window. The Birdman tries to tell it why it should go, leave him. His voice gets dreamy, full of wonder. He tells the bird that out there it can kick up the dust, it can dance to fiddle music, watch the alfalfa bloom. Breathing's easy outside, and nights move faster, but still the bird won't fly. Finally he asks the sparrow to go out there for him. Bite the stars, for him. And the bird flies through the bars. The Birdman sits on the edge of his bunk, that same look of gladness and pain on his face because he loved it, and he let it go, doesn't want the sparrow to ever come back.

The roads were slippery, headlights from oncoming cars shone blinding stars in my eyes. It got to be hypnotizing and I had to blink to keep myself from staring into the lights and veering into them, watch the road ahead. The whoosh of the wipers on the windshield back and forth in my ears was the sound of blood pumping. Slick black night, black rain, white-knuckled driving for home, telling myself nothing was there to scare me. Nothing was hiding in the dark but the dark itself.

I was thinking about the Birdman when he told his wife it was his life sentence, not hers. But their lives were joined, I thought, how could she go dance? How could the bird fly away? Maybe by biting the stars, only then something of both lives was let soar.

The tires skidded on the wet pavement, losing their grip on the curves, and I clenched the wheel praying they'd keep to the road. The wipers gave me seconds of clarity. I could see nothing was in front of me but the long way back. When I pulled into the drive, I cut the ignition and laid my forehead on the steering wheel. Then a loud rap on my window, a shining badge the rain fell on. Two men wearing suits, tired of waiting for me half the night. I thought there was something to be afraid of in the dark. I got out of my car.

"Grace Larson." One of them said my name, the worst I'd ever heard it said.

I held my purse against my chest. A raindrop caught my eyelash. "Yes."

"You're out late. Mind if we ask you where you've been?"

Another raindrop rolled down my cheek but I didn't care to wipe it away, more were falling.

SPIDER WEBS

Spiders use several strategies to capture prey: active hunting, waiting in ambush, and making and using traps of silk. The most distinctive strategy is the use of the silk orb web. Spider silk is made of protein strands. It is twice as strong for its size as steel, and able to stretch up to 30 percent before breaking. Orb webs have strong support threads for the frame, like girders that join to a central point. Concentric rings of sticky silk create the catching surface. The spider often sits at the hub of the web, with each of its legs on a different radiating thread. When a prey is caught it feels the vibrations. In mythology, the web represents fate. A fly trapped in the web is help-less to escape its fate.

FOURTEEN

Jess was dead nearly five years, grass grown long around his grave. The stone marker already moss-covered and shifted in the ground, one side sunk deeper than the other. His sleep restless below the earth. And Cole, restless above.

He wasn't stunt-riding motorcycles anymore, but he was still traveling around, wandering with the wind. He was in and out of jail, in and out of my life. When he came home, I'd find a string of blood on my bathroom mirror. By then he was a heroin addict. Tiny specks sprayed on the glass after he shot his arm full of dope. My boy careless with his blood, wasting himself with a needle. I'd wipe away the chain of red dots but later they'd be there again. My face in the mirror wiping the glass clean of my child's lost blood.

Cole had a record of robberies, possession of narcotics and stolen property. I'd watch TV and hear about some crime, wonder did he do it? I'd be in my chair in the living room at night, and where was he — climbing in a window of a dark house, rolling a car down a street, lights off, its engine silent.

Sometimes a program showed a reenactment of a crime with actors playing the roles of the bandit and the victims. Sometimes an actor looked like Cole. I'd see him in a bank reaching into his jacket and pulling out a gun. He'd draw down on a row of bodies on the floor, ladies with their skirts twisted exposing their upper thighs in pantyhose, feet splayed in pumps. The camera would focus on the bank security guard as he bravely stands from his desk, rising like a country's flag, zoom to the terror in his eyes, his gray hair, his hand's slow reach for the gun in his holster, the wedding band on his finger. He'd be so very careful because he was the only hope of a hero anybody had, and he knew it. He'd try but he wouldn't be quiet enough. The bandit would turn, wild rage cramping his face, point the gun at the guard's head. Close in then on the eyes — those of a scared grandfather and those of a madman. The guard lets go of the idea of getting his weapon and saving anyone, lifts his hands in the air beside his face as it's blown off. The bandit — Cole? — grabs the duffel bag of cash from the teller and runs out the doors down the sidewalk. The bank customers shift on the floor like they are waking, begin to move, but the security guard does not. He does not move, nor does the camera. Mercifully he is lying face down, a bloody halo around his gray head.

I imagined then the lead actors taking off their wardrobe — the security uniform, beat-up leather jacket — and putting on their own clothes again to go home. They might leave the studio together, walk out side by side, share a joke in the parking lot. They could do that because it wasn't real to them, they were acting. They could change clothes and be somebody else. At the end of the program, there was a number to call if you had any information about the crime which might lead to the arrest of a suspect. If you had a clue who he was.

It could have been Cole. It could have not been. The image of my son waving the gun at those people wouldn't leave my head. It looked like my son, and seeing him with my own eyes like that made it not such a far stretch to believe it was him. Not when it's played out in front of you. There it is. Can you believe your eyes?

Cole met Ivy then and married her, though he had a bevy of girlfriends to choose from. I don't think he gave them all up right away either. More than once Ivy called me looking for him. Sometimes he'd be gone from her all night, sometimes nights in a row. She guessed he was with another woman, but she wasn't sure — if he was strung out somewhere, or locked up? She hated having to dial me, call his mother to see if I knew where he was.

"I can't stand it," she'd tell me into the phone.

"He's not easy to keep track of, but he loves you," I'd say.

"You think? Lucky me."

Married or not, Cole liked to party and he liked to flirt with women, and it caused a rift between them from the start. Ivy had an idea she could change him. I didn't blame her for wanting to try. I had hopes riding on it she could. I wanted her love to build a bridge for Cole, let him walk over it to the other side where the grass was greener. But Cole didn't know about a bridge. He wanted a doormat, and if Ivy wouldn't let him wipe his feet on her, he'd find a welcome mat somewhere else.

I drove to Ellen's one weekend to visit with her. Ronny was at a convention and the boys were gone all over the country guiding adventure tours. They whitewater rafted, climbed ice-capped mountains, skied straight vertical slopes after jumping out helicopters. Ellen was by herself like I was and we spent the weekend together cooking meals and going for walks. We sat at dusk watching the sky turn color, the sun blaze lower and lower until it got cold and dark and we had to put on sweaters, tuck our feet under us, watch the stars come out.

Ellen told me she was worried about her boys, the risks they were taking, accidents they could have, danger that might find them. "Think of it, they could break a leg. Or they could hit their head on a rock and drown in a river. They might be swallowed in an avalanche." She wrapped her arms around herself. "I'm out of my mind with worry."

Her night-blooming flowers were perfuming the air, a bed of pretty, white-flowering tobacco. She went on, "They hardly ever call. I only get postcards."

"They send me postcards too," I told her. "I have them on my fridge. I think they're having fun." Her boys weren't hurting anybody else, I wanted to tell her. They weren't the avalanche that could ice somebody under.

"I just miss them," she said. "Well, you know."

I came back and Cole had been at the house, used it to party since I was gone. He'd left a mess of crushed beer cans, dirty dishes, unmade beds. Ivy wouldn't let him carry on at their place so I guess he'd been happy to find my house black, empty, just how he liked it. I went around opening the windows to air it out, throwing things into a trash bag. I threw the ashtrays in with the ashes, plates, glasses, bedsheets, pillow cases. I didn't want them. I didn't want this. I had the locks changed on the doors.

One night after that I was in bed and I heard Cole outside screaming for me. Screaming *Mama* in the dark, all these years after he was grown into a man. I found him laying in the grass in the yard. His voice by then had gone hoarse, and his mouth was white, frothy with spit, his chin shiny with drool. His hair was wet, plastered lankly to his skull. He scared me. He thrashed his head from side to side, his hands holding his stomach, tucking in at the waist, his legs drawing up then kicking out again. He was sobbing, worked himself up to another scream even though I was there.

"Shhh," I told him. I covered his mouth with my palm. "Okay." I leaned in, pressing my lips to the back of my own hand as I held it there. I looked into my son's eyes that close and he was looking back at me. But I know he didn't see but the demons in his head. "I'm right here," I said.

"Mama?"

"I'm here."

"You got to help me!" His body twisted into itself, writhing as though he had a hook through the middle. He grabbed at my clothes with his clawed fists.

"What is it? Are you hurt?" I thought I knew that it was the drugs, the heroin.

"It hurts bad." His teeth were gritted. "You got to get me some. Oh, Mama."

He was shaking and I looked at the whole of his body, checking for blood, an injury or wound on the outside that would cause this. But there was nothing. He had blood coming out of his nostrils, mixing with the spit around his mouth.

"Get me some!" He went on mumbling and clutching at his stomach, groaning like he was on a bed of razors instead of blades of soft grass. A lightning bug blinked near him, a tiny green light winking out. There was a gun tucked under Cole's belt, hard steel against his clenching stomach muscles. The sight of both together scared me worse.

"I'm dying, Mama," he said. "Help me." His face collapsed with the pain. Tears came to my eyes seeing him like that. "Fuck," he howled, angry. He gnashed his teeth, tossed his head. A devil had him, the fight was inside.

"Hold my hand," I said. "Hold it tight." He squeezed my hand in a vise lock, grinding the knuckles together so I cried out. "That's it," I said, "you just hold on." He was moaning slightly, but he'd stilled to hard shaking, his teeth chattering.

"You got to get to the other side of this," I told him. I thought of giving birth, the pain, pushing through it to hold my baby in my arms. "There's not another way."

His eyes rolled white but he kept hold of my hand. "This will all get out of your system. Hear me. You're going to be clean."

His body coiled rigid then pulled in fetal, struck out. It took all his supply of energy to yell, "Get me some, Mama! Help me." Then he sobbed hopelessly again. "Fucking bitch," he said. "Why won't you help me? I hate you. Why do you hate me?" All through his tears.

He was on his side and I rubbed his back in circles, stroking the damp cloth of his T-shirt the way I used to when I put him to sleep as a child. "Hush," I said. He was shivering in a cold sweat. "Can we try and get you in the house? Help me stand you up."

He coughed, a choking spasm that caused him to bring up bile. I wiped his mouth with my dress, smoothed the hair from his forehead. He couldn't be moved yet. I laid down beside him. I whispered, *The Lord is my shepherd, I shall not want. He maketh me to lie down in green pastures.* "This is your green pasture," I told Cole.

In the sky hung a strange red moon that night. Up there all kinds of seas. The Sea of Rains, Sea of Clouds, Sea of Serenity, Sea of Crises. All those seas, but not a single drop of water. Cole went in and out of sleep until I managed to get him lifted up, he half walked was half dragged, into the house.

He could swallow and keep down but thin soup at first, I spooned into him myself. Sometimes he talked like he was possessed, acted like it, growling and rabid. He soaked the bedsheets with sweat, then needed a pile of blankets to keep him warm. I sat at the kitchen table while he slept, drinking coffee, so full of despair I was numb.

I sponged Cole's chest and back in the bed as best I could, laid a washcloth over his face, even though in his delirium he fought me off. He struck out at me and bruised my arm. He cringed at my touch as if fire ants were crawling under his skin. As the days went by, color came back to his complexion and I brought a razor and a bowl of water to shave his growth of beard.

It was a strange thing to do, shave my son's face. I hadn't touched his cheek, his chin, his jaw, his neck — for how long? Cole kept his eyes closed and I let myself revel in the details of him close up, all I could see. I used my hand to check if the skin was smooth, swishing the blade clean in the water bowl. He opened his eyes and it startled me. I smiled and he put his finger to the scar on my lip. He did it the way a blind person might, feel something but not be certain what to make of it. I thought maybe he was sorry. He wished I could look at him without part of my smile holding back.

He was skinny and weak, his cheeks hollow under the bone, cords of veins stood out on his arms and the backs of his hands. There was an intensity to him, though. He looked hard underneath, like a dare.

Ivy called and he spoke to her on the phone and I knew she was telling him to come back, let her take care of him. But he seemed unwilling yet to make a move to go anywhere. He wasn't ready to leave. He played his old drums and he slept and he watched TV. Ivy called again. I tried to add my voice to hers, get him to go home. I thought it was time. But he was hiding, that was the truth. He was afraid to leave my house. Even if restlessness was growing in him. He'd spring out of a chair, throw himself on the floor do a set of push-ups. He wasn't as weak as he looked.

Maybe he didn't trust himself back in the world, the temptations there. This was time away from time, limbo. It wasn't real.

"Don't you miss Ivy?" I said to him.

He didn't answer.

"Nobody's making you do anything you don't want. You have choices. Your life is your own."

"Right, Mama." But his eyes flashed — what did I know? What did I know about moves he could make, if he hadn't made his choices already and now it just had to play out?

Then for two nights in a row he took his sleeping bag outside and slept in the yard. From the kitchen, I'd see the lit end of his cigarette burning in the dark, the arc to his lips like the trail of a shooting star. It was like he used to do — laid with his hands behind his head, gazing up at the sky, the array of stars, heaven way off. It must have seemed like that to him — he was a speck in the universe. The next day he was gone with the light.

Ivy told me he called her, wanted her to come meet him. He went straight to his dealer to buy heroin. He pumped a hit into his arm, only sure way he knew to get to heaven. She found him, the needle dangling from his vein. He took a ride to the stars, shooting like a comet, burning out across the sky.

Ivy didn't know what to do with Cole any more than I did. "I don't have your patience, Grace. I hate loving him."

I still saw Harlin on Tuesdays at the library, our sanctuary. We sat under the pecan tree. Drugs were something Harlin could talk about after his tour in Vietnam. He didn't let me be ashamed, I could tell him anything I needed to, anything was on my mind, he'd hear it. I told him Cole was a junkie. His marriage with Ivy was in trouble, he had no ambition, he was dangerous. To himself and others. He'd added an assault charge to his record. At least in jail he'd get straight. But Harlin said there was better stuff inside than could be bought on the street. Whatever Cole wanted — amphetamines, barbiturates, even heroin — he could get, no problem. Bars didn't keep anything out.

More and more Cole's life orbited around his drug habit. Getting the money for a fix, shooting up, getting more money. He was reckless, spent longer at a time in jail.

It took a toll on Ivy. She'd quit work and come home to their apartment not knowing what she'd find — if Cole would even be there, or be OD'd, or throwing a party, or back in jail. She took to visiting him less when he was locked up. She didn't like being inside the walls of the jail. She didn't like the whole process of getting in to see her husband. She had better things to do than waste her time with him when he was too stoned to talk to her and make sense.

I sat there often enough feeling the same thing. It didn't seem he was at all willing to help himself. He got into fights while he was behind bars, bad behavior lost him good time, delayed his parole. Ivy was getting tired of waiting. One time Cole sat with me clutching his sides like he was freezing cold, he had cracked his ribs in a fight. Even the air hurt him to breathe. He said he'd pushed a man's teeth down his throat.

"The asshole'll be shitting teeth for a week. Get it, Mama?"

I looked at the floor like maybe I'd dropped something, or a hole would open and I'd fall through to the other side of the world. The China of my childhood, so far everything was faded either red or white, the feathers on the strange birds, the long silk robes, even the distant snow-capped mountains.

"It's funny, Mama," he said.

I didn't know what to think anymore in his defense. I fought not to give up on him. Heroin was a demon inside him, I'd seen it with my own eyes, frothing out of his mouth. There were other demons too that I'd never see, but didn't mean they weren't tearing him up from within. I wouldn't let that tornado come back for him, in its fury pull him from my grasp. I would hold on.

I went to the jail on the set days and times for visits. The more crowded it was, the less time you had that day. Cole knew some of the inmates from other stints inside, and it could be a social club in the visiting gallery, which was like a big cafeteria with long rows of tables, fluorescent lights, and vending machines.

A visitor was allowed to bring ten dollars in coins for the machines. It was against the rules for the inmates to put the money in the slots themselves. They had to stand beside you and tell you what they wanted. They would point to gum, or a candy bar, or a bag of chips. Then while you pushed the buttons and got it for them, they'd wait with their arms hanging at their sides. You had to take the snack out from where it dropped behind the low plastic window, and hand it to them. I spent all the money getting Cole a heap of chocolate bars which he'd eat one after the other until only the empty wrappers were in front of us.

Visits weren't a natural way to sit and talk. It was like making you drink when you weren't thirsty. Sometimes we had nothing to talk about, or nothing that seemed worth saying. Cole would eat his candy bars and look around the room, and I'd look at him. Then in a while, maybe one of us would be moved to say something.

"You should see my tomatoes," I might say. "I don't think they've ever been bigger. They're like baby heads, as heavy as that, and pretty."

"Yeah?" Cole would say.

"They taste good too. I've been eating them everyday. There are all kinds of ways to eat a tomato. You can eat them just raw. You don't need salt."

The most talking we did after a while was inside the walls of a correctional institution. Not for a minute did we ever forget where we were. Our words knocked around the walls looking for a way out, a way to rise above, but they never did break free.

Cole called me from jail on the phone. It could be harder for me to only hear his voice in my ear. The silences seemed longer, his tone flat, or ranting about some injustice done to him by another inmate. The phone ringing in my quiet house could fill me with dread. I'd look at the phone like a snake. I had to make myself reach and pick it up, tell myself it wouldn't bite. There wasn't much I could do for Cole when he was locked behind bars. Nothing I could do to change that. I could buy him candy from the vending machines when I saw him to visit. And I could make sure when he called me on the phone I was at the other end of the line to pick up.

Ivy did visit him sometimes but it was hard on her. She would drive all the way there, only to find he'd had his visiting privileges suspended for some trouble he'd been in. She'd have to turn around and drive all the way back. The conversation she'd planned, words she'd rehearsed in the car, flew out the window. She hated it. But the more Ivy kept her distance from him, the wilder he went for her, more he tried to keep her under his thumb.

The last long stretch Cole was out, they were at each other's throats until Ivy went to stay with her mother. He sweet-talked her back, but in less than a week, Ivy caught him going through her purse, looking for drug money. He found something he liked better. Cole held the bottle of Valium up out of her reach.

She told him to give it back. She had tears in her eyes. Which I bet Cole thought he could understand. He wouldn't want to give up the Valium either, if it belonged to him.

It didn't matter what she said to him then, he didn't hear. She pleaded again that it was hers, would he give it back to her, please? But he wouldn't. All he saw was the word on the prescription, what it meant to him, and Ivy was muted to his ears.

She couldn't get through to explain to him it wasn't what he thought. Finally Cole took the lid off, shook some out into his hand. He yelled at her, wanted to know what the fuck this was about? She told him. It was her baby teeth.

He threw the fistful at her, then he threw the bottle. Little ivory teeth scattered across the floor like a broken strand of pearls.

Ivy, the child beauty queen, got down on her hands and knees to pick them up, put them back in the jar. Cole watched her, still not believing his bad luck.

She found the teeth one by one, blew the dust off them, and dropped them into the prescription bottle with a tiny clink. As a child, she'd thought the tooth fairy had taken them from under her pillow, flown off with them, each tooth held like a jewel in delicate fairy hands, been thrilled in the morning to find a quarter when she slipped her hand under the cool belly of the pillow. But they hadn't gone to fairyland. Her mama had saved them, every one, treasured them more than any fairy could. She'd saved them for her daughter, now grown, a gift of childhood magic. A jar full of love.

Cole crouched down beside his wife. He picked up a tooth. It was almost purely white, but translucent. It was even tinier than a pill, hollow at its core, but hard as a diamond. He held it out to Ivy, impossibly small between his thick fingers.

She swatted his hand away. She hit his arm, she hit his chest, his head. Hit him over and over until the baby teeth scattered again from the bottle and she threw it back at him, spilling everything that had been inside it.

FIFTEEN

Cole chased Ivy like a shadow. He wouldn't let her be. That's how he knew to love her. But it didn't feel like romance to Ivy, it felt like hounding. If he wasn't on her tail, he was off on another scent. Ivy caught him in their bed with somebody else. She was working then taking tickets at a movie theater and was gone most nights. Most but not all. This night she had promised to get off early, before the late show, and bring home some wine, they'd order Chinese and be together. It was her birthday. Cole didn't remember. The woman in their bed was too stoned to get out of it. Ivy had the box from the supermarket with her birthday cake in it held up to throw at them, but she didn't. They hardly knew she was standing there. She put the box on the floor and went out.

She got in her car and started to drive, no plan in her mind to ever turn around and come back. The only regret she'd have, that she didn't kick the cake box flying. She was done with Cole. She drove with the radio on, open road ahead of her. But then she pulled over to the side, and looked in the rearview. She saw there was nothing behind her, nothing to go back to, and she turned the car around anyway. She saw her eyes in the mirror looking at herself, the way she'd looked at herself on her wedding day in her new husband's sunglasses. She didn't like what she saw but she drove back. She drove to my house. She wanted me to explain to her why she'd married a bank robber.

"You're his mother," she told me. "Tell me what I was thinking."

We were sitting in the backyard, her eyes red from crying.

"I'm not a bad person," she said. "If I see a turtle on the road, I stop and pick it up, bring it back to the grass. Coming here I saved two turtles from getting hit by cars. I even stopped to save a clump of dirt."

"I don't know," she said. She took a sip of lemonade from the glass I'd set beside her. "What did I expect? Everybody warned me not to take up with him," she said. "I thought I saw something in him. What did I see? He had his eyes hid behind those shades."

She looked down at her hands in her lap. I noticed she wasn't wearing her wedding ring. Maybe she was noticing that too. I wondered if Cole had pawned it.

"Well, nothing's perfect is it?" she said. "You're his mother, I shouldn't complain to you." She gave me a weak smile.

I returned her smile, covering the scar on my mouth so that no part of it held back, the best I could do. "I used to imagine having a daughter," I told her. "If it would be different than a son? I thought we might see the world through similar eyes. But then I think of my mama and my sister. None of us can hope to look out at the world from inside anybody else. We can only ever look from the outside, no matter how close we get. We're on the outside. Nothing is perfect, Ivy. But you deserve to be happy."

Her chin trembled. "I want to be happy." She said it in a small voice, like a wish.

I wanted to tell her she would be, all her dreams would come true. I brought the lemonade up to my lips, the glass so cold in my hand it was wet with tears on the outside.

"Look," Ivy said. "Cole bought me a present, for my birthday. He put it in the glove compartment, I wouldn't have found it if I wasn't looking for a kleenex to dry my eyes when I was leaving him. Or was it when I turned around to come back? He wrapped it in tin foil." She took a little parcel out of her purse.

"Why don't you open it?" I said.

"There was a note too with it. I already opened that. You know what it said, Grace? *Dear Ivy, Happy birthday. You are for me. Anyways and always, C.J.*" She looked at me blankly. "You are for me," she repeated. "And instead of where a bow should be on top of the present, he taped a cash register receipt there. See? Nine dollars and change." She flicked the corner of the paper ticket with her finger. "You are for me," she said again. "What do you think that means?"

"It means you are the one for him. He loves you."

"Or else I belong to him, like *you are mine.*"

"No. It means you're the one."

"But not the only one," Ivy said softly.

I wanted to tell her something different. "You're the only one he loves," I said. "You're his wife."

"Maybe," she said. She was still flicking the cash receipt with her fingertip.

I told her, "A long time ago, Ivy, I accused Cole of stealing something he gave me for my birthday. A pair of slippers and some cologne. He wants you to know that he thought of you, in a moment when you weren't there. You were on his mind and it was worth something to him. He was willing to pay money to buy you a present because you have value to him. You being happy was worth more than money in his pocket."

"I was worth nine dollars to him?" she said. But it was just words. She opened the wrapping slowly and with care. She held up a little plastic pouch. A beauty kit that contained a bottle of red nail polish, a matching lipstick, and a folding mirror. She took the lid off the tube of lipstick. She raised her eyebrow. "It's red alright," she said. But she lifted the mirror and rolled the color on her lips. Then she gingerly untaped the bill from the tin foil and tucked it in her purse. "Guess I'll be going now," she said. "It's hard to know."

It wasn't until that night when I was getting ready for bed I saw her goodbye kiss on my cheek. Sweetly bright and hopeful. I was careful to wash around it, laid my head on the pillow on the other side not to smudge it. I wanted it to last.

A few weeks later Ivy quit work and came out of the movie theater, found Cole smoking under the marquee. She was still wearing the red lipstick, had worn it every day, and Cole pressed his mouth to hers. She said right then she got a bad feeling in the pit of her stomach and braced herself. His kiss was hard. She could feel the electric shocks on her skin, blue sparks being near him. He was charging the air with static. "Let's go for a ride," he said.

They walked to her car, Cole's arm draped around the back of her neck, dead weight on her shoulders. Usually he wanted to drive so she passed him the keys, but he tossed them back to her, went around to the passenger side.

"You drive," he said, spiked his cigarette into the gutter.

He beat his fingers on the dash, drumming in time to the music cranked on the radio. He was vibrating beside her.

"Where do you want to go?" she asked him.

"Why not Memphis? We could hear a band."

"I'm kind of tired," Ivy said.

"Why don't we make out somewhere?"

"Let's go home then."

"Naw."

They ended up making love in the car on a residential street. Cole was too high for much. He was in his own world. After, he got out of the car and peed into a row of hedges.

"Let's go," he said.

"Where?"

"Just drive." His voice cut, a steel edge in the air.

Ivy tried to make conversation, but he turned up the volume on the radio. "Prick," she said. He turned it up louder still. She shook her head.

Cole directed her where to go but he didn't seem to have a plan, pointed out turns, left, right, on his whim. They came to a dead end and Ivy drove right to the end of it, the last of the pavement. "There's no more road," she said. "I want to go home."

He studied her. His eyes were black, all the color gone from them. There was only night in them now, only the dark. "Sure," he said, and he didn't even blink. "I need to get a pack of smokes first."

As she was driving back, he motioned to a convenience store, told her to pull in front. "I'll be right out," he said. "Keep the motor running."

She waited. On his seat was a pack of Camels. She picked it up and felt the weight of it, slid open the top and saw it was nearly full. Her throat tightened closed. She looked into the window of the convenience store, saw Cole and the clerk on either side of the counter. Nothing more than that, but she shifted the car into drive. She thought she saw something in Cole, something in the way he was standing maybe, the tilt of his head. She put her foot down on the accelerator just as Cole grabbed hold of the door handle and jumped in beside her. She hit the brakes.

ELIZA CLARK

"What the fuck —!" he yelled at her. "Move!"

She ignored him. He shot his leg over the stick shift and floored the gas. They rocketed forward, tires squealing. Ivy lifted her hands off the steering wheel and put them over her eyes. The car swerved towards the curb. Cole snatched control of the wheel at the same time he climbed into the driver's seat, pushing her out of the way behind him. He drove crazy. Even when it seemed they'd safely gotten away, he gunned the engine. Ivy hollered to let her out, threatened to dive out. Finally, she leaned back and kicked Cole in the side, winding him. The car veered into a pole. Ivy's head hit the windshield and bounced back. Cole's wrist was fractured, but still he managed to shove Ivy's body back into the driver's seat, take off running. That early hour of the morning, it was a while before anybody got there to help.

Ivy'd been knocked unconscious and taken to the hospital. She didn't tell how the accident happened and nobody asked. Maybe the doctors figured she didn't remember why she crashed, or how she got so out of control. It was true, she didn't. It all spun away from her. She was confused. Why, was hard. She'd have to stand back and look at the whole picture, she was still too close to see it. When Ivy bothered to put lipstick on, could tell them her name and her address, and seemed to know where she was going, they released her.

Ivy cried when Cole was arrested. I think she cried for herself as much as anything else. She knew this was how it would always be with him. A heavy knock on the door, clatter of steel handcuffs, neighbors peering into the hallway, and after, walking through her like she was invisible, or dirt under their shoes.

The police came and waited while Cole put on his hightops with the velcro straps. In jail they would take the laces from his shoes, take his belt. They were his jail shoes he put on. Cole was arrested on a burglary charge, a different crime than the convenience store, which went unsolved. Though it wasn't a serious charge in itself, because he had a growing long record, he could have drawn a harsher sentence for it. Probation was possible, but maybe not likely, depending on the judge.

Ivy missed him when he was gone, despite herself. I think in her mind, she tried to tell herself love could bend steel bars. Cole would've liked to see that happen. She tried to pretend the glass wall wasn't there between them when she went to visit him. One time, Cole came in the room and sat down on the other side of the glass, Ivy pounded her fist on it. Then she couldn't pretend it didn't keep them apart. All Cole did was put his hand flat against the glass, and let her pound until she was done. I think she tried to tell herself things would change. He would. But another part of her had backed away already, had turned to face her own future, clearly looming.

I could see her future too. She had a future and she would move towards it if she let herself. What next? It was something I hadn't allowed myself to think about, I kept to the present. Not that you can ever really guess what next, but maybe you still need to cast yourself forward, hope something worthwhile will be there when you get to it.

I went to visit Cole while he waited to find out what his sentence would be. He'd tattooed H-A-R-D L-U-C-K on his knuckles. I made him lift up his hands to show me. Luck. After the tornado touched down on our church, there was talk of luck, lucky this didn't happen or that didn't. Lucky it wasn't worse. It could always be worse. I felt lucky Cole was born, when all those pretty little girls lost their lives under the church roof. Maybe they were lucky they didn't suffer more. It happened fast. But I remember the mother bent over her daughter, forcing her own breath into the girl's lungs as if she could live for her. Luck was hard, Cole was right.

I wanted my son to make some plans for himself. I tried to get him to see this was his one shot at his life, not we're cats who have lives to spare, can die and not be dead. But the way he looked at me from beyond the glass — maybe I didn't know what I was talking about, didn't know about walking dead.

After I left that day, Cole stuck a guard on the grounds with a sharpened metal pipe. Escaped, to chase after Ivy. He thought he'd escaped. He was hoping his luck would change. As he ran, maybe he thought it had, maybe he was running for the future — running for his life.

But the ink was under his skin. From then, all he had to do wherever he went after that was look down and read the way it was. It couldn't change.

TURTLES

Turtles rely on their hard shells for protection against predators. The shell is made up of two layers. An inner, bony layer, and an overlapping horny layer of shields. When it needs to defend itself, a turtle will pull its head into the shell by retracting its neck into an S-shaped curve. An air pump at the base of the neck allows it to breathe, since its rib cage is fused to its shell and can't expand to draw air. The lines visible on the surface of the shell reveal the turtle's age, though time may make them blur.

SIXTEEN

The police detectives sat at my kitchen table drying the rain-water off them with dish towels. The middle of the night, only the yellow glare of the ceiling fixture above, the house dark around us, the world dark outside. My hair and clothing were rain dampened, my legs tired-aching as I stood making coffee at the counter. The black dog barked, paced a circle, and flopped on the floor with a thud. I thought of the spirit circles I'd read about once, drawn to keep demons away. Inside the ring, was it formed of chalk or dried herbs or crystal rocks, no harm could come to you. The circle was a safe haven. If I could just lay beside the dog in that ring he'd traced on the floor, and sleep without fear.

Instead I ran water into the kettle, set it on the stove to boil. I put a spoonful of instant coffee into each of the three mugs in a row on the counter. I kept my back to the men. They'd introduced themselves as Detectives Wallace and de la Houssaye, a Cajun with a slow flow of words, black hair, and a shadow of beard already since it was almost morning. It was Wallace, whose voice was curt, did most of the talking. They wanted to ask me some questions about my son. Talk to me about where he was.

"Do I need to call a lawyer?"

They said I didn't need to bother, they just had some questions to ask, that was all. They had a search warrant, wanted to look in Cole's room.

"You won't find him there," I said.

"No, ma'am," Wallace said. "We didn't expect to." He gave de la Houssaye a look, a smile in it at my expense. Then he regarded me coolly. De la Houssaye seemed gentler in his manner, to me he did, he'd folded the dish towel over his knee instead of bunching it on the table when he was done using it. He didn't have the same look of spite in his eyes.

The kettle cried and I got up, poured the water into the coffee. The rain hammered on the roof louder suddenly, the storm far from abating, the sky opening up. I put a mug of steaming coffee in front of each of them and sat down, my legs so tired they started to buckle early and I had to grip the table rim, lower myself awkwardly. I realized I'd forgotten to bring my own mug over and glanced to where it was still on the counter. De la Houssaye saw me look and went and brought it to me. I clasped my hands around the mug, not trusting they could lift it without it would spill. Really it was too burning hot to hold, but I didn't let go.

I thought of what Jackson had told me about how people who were caught in house fires would grab hold of a metal doorknob to get out of a room. Their palm would melt to it, seared by the heat. They were supposed to know to touch the door first, check how hot it was. They were supposed to know that if the doorknob melted their hand, if they opened the door they'd be walking into fire. But all they wanted was out. It was instinct, pull open a door and run, even if it was the last thing they did.

"Your son's in a lot of trouble," Wallace said. "I guess I don't need to tell you that."

I noticed I hadn't put out the cream and sugar bowl either on the table, but I didn't care if they had to drink their coffee black, if it was so bitter they couldn't swallow it down. I didn't care.

"We think you know where Cole is," Wallace said. His voice was grim, firm. "He's facing hard time in prison now. I guess you know that too. We want you to tell us where he is before it gets any worse for him."

I shook my head. "Why would I? This might be my son's only chance. He can start over."

I'd made him angry. He set his jaw. De la Houssaye looked away from me. "It's not that simple. He's got debts to pay. He's an escaped convict, do you understand that? Do you understand he seriously injured a correctional officer? Know this, if we have to go after him, hunt him down, I promise you your son will be sorry."

"What if he's already sorry?" I said.

"The only thing he can do right now is turn himself in, do his time, pay out his debts, then he's free to start over."

"I think he thinks he's free now."

"You're not hearing. We will go after him, Mrs. Larson, and we will catch him. If your son tries to run we will shoot him. Do you understand?"

I couldn't have spoken then if I wanted to.

Wallace said, "Do you get what I'm saying? Tell us where he is before it's too late."

I had my head lowered looking down into the black coffee in my mug. I saw my reflection in the liquid dark, wavering.

"You know you can be arrested for harboring a fugitive." Wallace pushed in towards me across the table. "Tom Betts, that was the name of the guard your son stabbed. He had twin baby girls at home, two years old, came up just to his knees. He used to lift them in the air, one in each arm. Now they come and stand in front of him with their hands above their heads wanting up, waiting for him to pick them up. He can't due to his injury." Wallace paused. "I think your son made those little girls his victims. He made them put their hands up in the air and get nothing for it."

De la Houssaye said, "How many victims are you willing to let there be?"

I pressed my fingers against my mouth. I thought he seemed sad, not just for the guard, or for his children, but for me, my child, this whole thing we were in. I looked into the black of my coffee cup. "What if Cole gives himself up?"

"Surrenders?" Wallace said. "Be clear."

"Can you arrange it?" de la Houssaye said.

I honestly didn't know. I didn't know if Cole shouldn't run to Mexico or Canada. If he shouldn't run for his life. "I don't know," I said. "I don't know what I'm saying."

That made Wallace angry again. "We'll get your son. You tell him that. One way or the other he's going to prison."

"Talk to Cole," de la Houssaye said. "See if you can convince him to turn himself in. The judge will take that into account."

"Do it soon," Wallace said. He put a card with his phone number on the table.

They stood up, showed me the warrant that meant they could search Cole's room, and went to do that, with the black dog loping after them. I stayed where I was. I heard drawers opening and closing, the sound of them talking. It seemed they were in there for hours. I laid my head on my arms and shut my eyes. When I woke up, Cole's room was empty, they were gone. The posters had been pulled off his walls, baring the holes he'd made with his fists, like so many screaming mouths.

I let the dog out into the yard. I watched as he relieved himself on the chinaberry tree then put his nose to the ground and sniffed around, rooting up bugs in the grass, eating them like popcorn. I ought to give him a name at least. Tom Betts, that was a name. Cole James Larson. I named him for nobody but himself. Now they were linked. In my mind, in news reports. When I heard Cole's name on the television news, or read it in the paper, it was always his full name. As though by listing it all, Cole James Larson, they believed they had got all of him. They thought they had captured him.

I loaded the dog into the back seat of the car and wondered if I would be followed. I planned to drive out of town to a pay phone and tell Cole what the detectives had said. I don't know how many pay booths I passed and didn't stop at. I drove for miles. I had no idea where I was going, what I would say to Cole when he picked up the phone. What was best to advise him? Give himself up or run and never look back? I thought of Tom Betts and his baby girls, I thought of Ivy. What was best for my boy? I drove on until I couldn't not hear the black dog whining in the back, wanting out of the car.

Where I took us was to the shady pond Jackson and I had gone swimming in the summer we met. It was secluded as I remembered it, those big old willows still clinging to its banks. Same flat water, same grass we laid ourselves down on. The black dog thought he'd found a paradise, raced ahead of me into the water, splashing and barking for joy. Maybe he was some kind of water dog. He swam out of the water, shook himself off, plunged in again, keeping his head up, looking blissful. I tried not to think of my childhood puppy, how I wore him out believing it wasn't just me having fun. Loving him to death.

I sat with my back against a tree watching him. He was all I had for company. He couldn't help me know what to do about Cole. I hadn't told anybody, not Harlin or Mrs. B, not Ellen, nobody I could talk to, that I knew where Cole was hiding. I wouldn't jeopardize them, it wasn't fair, or Cole either. Last time I saw Harlin, he gave me that long straight stare of his.

"What's going on?" he asked me, holding his look, it dug deep.

I couldn't tell him. I think he was hurt by that, and I almost made something up to spare his feelings. It hurt me to not tell him, but I wouldn't lie.

"My friend," I said. "You know I love you?"

His eyes were calm. "You honor me, Grace." They were warm.

I'd read to him about the northern lights. Magnetic storms that were the result of electric currents triggered by the solar wind. The aurora looked like swirling cosmic flowers. A light storm of dark beauty.

From the edge of the pond, the black dog came bounding at me full speed, water flying off him, his ears silky wings. He came skidding to halt, planted his legs solid and shook, us both squinting our eyes against the sparkling spray of water, the drops like diamond starlights.

I stood and slipped off my shoes, unbuttoned my dress and hung it over a tree branch like I had those long years before. I let my underclothes fall to the ground. I walked barefoot to the pond, the dog already ahead of me dipping in the shallows. I waded into the cool water, out to the middle where it was as deep as my waist. I stood and cried. I didn't care anymore what the willows had to teach me about weeping without tears. I wept the only way I knew. Then I reached down to the mud bottom of the pond. I wiped mud over my chest. I took another handful and smeared it on my face, down my throat. I covered myself in mud, flowers of mud in my hair. When I was done, I looked up at the sky, I opened wide my arms and let myself fall back into the water.

The phone rang and rang, it rang off the hook. I was in a pay booth outside a gas station at the side of the road, my hair still dripping wet. Finally, when I was about to give up, somebody answered.

"Cole?" I said. The black dog was scampering around in the car, trying to stick his head out the partly opened window, barking. "It's me," I said.

"He's not here." It was a man's voice. Police? I wondered. I was gripping the receiver, but I thought to drop it and run.

"Can he come to the phone?" I said.

"No."

Not the police, they would try to draw me out, figure who I was, how I knew to call Cole there. "Who is this?" I said. The line went dead, lifeless in my hand.

I sat in the car staring down the road one way towards home, and the other direction that led to Cole's apartment. Nobody was supposed to know where he was. Who did the man's voice belong to? Anybody Cole figured he could trust enough to tell had to be somebody outside the law. That meant trouble. I didn't want to believe it. Cole drew trouble to him like a magnet. Why couldn't he come to the phone? Where was Ivy? I sat parked there at the crux, not knowing which way to turn. In the end, I headed home, the black dog long asleep on the back seat.

I spent the rest of the day outside in my garden, dividing clumps of peonies that were overcrowded and suffering for it. They weren't getting the light or the nutrients they needed to flower in their glory. I dug a deep moat around the base of each plant, lifted it from the earth and shook the dirt off the roots. Then with a sharp knife I cut them apart. A clean cut through the roots. It was the only way to give the flowers a chance to spread out and thrive. I tamped the earth back in place, stayed on my knees until the sun went down.

That night I called Cole again and got no answer. I called him from a roadside cafe. I sat in a leather booth drinking endless coffee, calling every hour, putting quarters in the phone and in the chrome jukebox at my table. I played Dusty Springfield and Willie Nelson, Waylon Jennings. The lyrics spoke to me. All those songs about love and loss, notes I knew by heart. When Dusty sang that just one smile, pain was forgiven, just one kiss and the hurt was gone, I knew what she meant. It was like a friend had laid a comforting hand on me.

I counted the rings until I lost count. Ringing in my ears and nobody picking up. Not even the man who'd answered before. I got in my car. The whole way I tried not to scare myself thinking about what I might find. Then I got a glimmer of hope. What if Cole and Ivy had left already, gone to Mexico or Canada? What if they were just gone, like that. Flying across state lines in a car with the windows down, or flying in a plane through the air. Or what if they weren't? Then what had happened to them?

I knocked on the apartment door and waited, then I opened it with my key. The lights were off and I found the switch, turned them on. The place was a mess. I called hello. It didn't seem to be anyone was home. I walked through, my footfalls on the wood floor, the refrigerator running the only sounds. The bedroom door was closed. I felt a punch of dread, knotted my stomach. I pushed the door open.

Ivy was on the bed. By the moonlight coming in the blinds I saw she was tied there, her hands caught to the headboard. It was slow motion getting to her, like wading through an ocean to get across the room, held back by the drag of the tide, nightmare of moving nowhere.

When she saw it was me, her eyes shut with relief, opened again full of tears. She watched my face. "It's okay," I said. "Oh

Ivy, it's alright now." I was untying the roped bandanna had been cutting her mouth to keep her from yelling. I unbound her wrists. As soon as I did, she sprang off the bed. She leapt off it like it was a bed of burning coals, like it was on fire. She tore the top she was wearing off over her head and threw it to the ground. She wrenched a shirt from its hanger in the closet, put it on, her hands shaking trying to do up the buttons. "I'm getting out of here," she said.

"What happened? Did Cole do this?"

She paused, her buttonholes gaping, then she unzipped her jeans and viciously kicked them off. She ripped a skirt from the clips of its hanger, put it on, made an effort to zip up the back, both her hands behind her back. "I'm getting the fuck out of here." She struggled some more with her zipper, tugging on it. "Fuck," she said. I went to help her, but at my touch she spun away.

"Where's Cole, Ivy?"

"Cole?" She jabbed his name back at me.

I nodded. I must have seemed pathetic to her, standing there in my worry and bewilderment. "I don't know what's happened," I said. I went and sat on the edge of the bed.

In a minute she came and sat beside me, all undone. She pushed her hands through her hair, then rested them in her lap, trying to calm herself. I saw her wrists where they'd been tied were scored deep red. I reached over and took one of her hands in mine and she let me. We stayed like that holding hands.

I said, "Please tell me what's going on?"

"Jesus," Ivy said.

"Please."

"Cole met this guy, somebody he knew from before. I don't know maybe from jail, or from hell. He kept pumping Cole full of shit. He was so strung out." She faced me then. "It wasn't

Cole tied me up. They were going to do a job. I heard them talking. Only Cole was so out of it. The guy had to keep repeating it, what they were going to do, rob a pharmacy. All the drugs they wanted, easy money on the street. Candy to a junkie." She buttoned her shirt from the bottom to the top. "I'm leaving, Grace," she said. And I knew she meant she was leaving Cole, leaving this all behind her.

"You go on," I said.

"Goddamn it," she said and left.

The door closed and fury rose in me, bitter taste in my mouth. Ivy tied to the bed. This was enough. Then I thought of Cole, just a little boy, tied to the bed at my sister Ellen's house. Tied so he couldn't prowl for the candy he wanted. I understood it, even if I couldn't bear to think he'd hurt himself if he was let to, he'd hurt anybody in his path.

I went to the phone and dialed the number on the card Wallace had put on my table. I told him I was giving him Cole. I told him what I knew about the job planned for the pharmacy.

"There was somebody with him," I said.

"Do you have a name?"

"No."

"A description?"

"No."

"If we had a name, we could check our files. It would give us something to go on."

"I only have a voice in my head sounding like trouble."

Neither of us said anything. Then I told Wallace, "I want you to understand this is a sacrifice. I'm giving you my boy, for his own good. Don't hurt him."

SEVENTEEN

If Cole had gone to Mexico. If he'd gone to Canada. If he'd done his time. I drove to the pharmacy. I wanted to be there, had to be, to give him up. My son. Surrender him so he could be saved. I would try to protect him if he couldn't protect himself. Draw a safe circle around him, concrete walls of a cell. Until he could step outside and no harm would come to him. But even then — would he do harm? The danger was inside him.

I met an undercover police agent a block from the pharmacy and he drove me in his car, as Wallace had arranged. The feeling I had, it was strange, I felt like I was in labor. A mix of fear and hope, anticipation of change, nothing would be the same again. Cole was inside the building. The police had stayed out of sight, watched from a distance as he broke the lock and went in. Then they'd positioned two vehicles at the rear exit, four to cover the front where Cole had gone in and where they expected he would come out. They didn't know a security guard was inside the pharmacy, hired for that night after the electronic security system went down. Cole's accomplice? Cole had gone in alone.

We drove to the edge of the parking lot and cut the engine, as close as we could be. In the darkness, I saw the four cars, side doors open, all lights out, for now, hiding. Officers were crouched in the shadows of their vehicles, using the doors as shields, waiting with their guns drawn. They had made their own circle, I thought, a circle of metal and guns. Cole inside it. A trap I'd fixed for him.

I rolled my window down, waited like they did, but I could just watch. Then Cole ran out the door. Lights shone on him. Blazing white lights all turned on him at once. The brightest lights I ever saw. Light of a million angels. Cole was blinded by them, his arm flew up to cover his eyes at the same time he fired his gun into the light. He looked full into a million suns and shot the light. He killed a police officer with a bullet to the head. Then he was fired on from the row of cars and he fell. I screamed his name. On the ground, I saw his head turn towards my voice. Lucky they'd only shot to bring him down.

I got out of the car and ran for him. An officer took hold of me, wouldn't let me go to him.

Most of the action was around the officer Cole had shot. He'd died instantly but still they tried to revive him. I watched as two of the men leaned over Cole where he was face down on the pavement, cuffed his hands behind his back, yanked him to his feet, careless of the bullet wound in his shoulder. I saw my son look at me. What was I doing here? did he wonder. Or did he put it together. His mother, the light firing back on him. Did he know it was for his own good? They pushed him into a car and sped away. He'd kicked the security guard unconscious inside the pharmacy.

At the penalty trial, the defense council presented a history of Cole's life. They wanted to provoke some sympathy in the jurors, some understanding. They started with his birth. There was evidence, they said, that biological factors might be responsible for his criminal behavior. A strong likelihood, because he was born prematurely, there was trauma resulting in oxygen deprivation which may have adversely affected the frontal cortex and the limbic system, causing abnormal brain activity. A neurosurgeon took the stand and told about electrical storms in the brain that cause inappropriate responses to impulses, violent episodes. The area of the brain that regulates moral behavior malfunctions and is the biological reason for the disorder of crime.

Some of what was said I didn't understand. But when I heard that Cole might have had storms in his head, I thought they were right. I'd always thought so. The tornado inside him. I was right. And I felt myself sit straighter for a time, thinking he wasn't bad, and I wasn't a bad mother. He had storms inside him. But then, in the end, it's what you do not who you are you're judged by. Not who you are inside.

They told about Cole being raised by a single mother, how he was yo-yoed from my sister's back to me. They brought up Jackson's suicide as a mitigating factor in his criminal history, how he got lost in a downward spiral after that. It sounded bleak as they meant it to, and I heard it like a drama of somebody else's life. They saw it different than I did. They didn't know all the whys of it. But more than once I cried for the boy they described, leading a life parallel to the one I thought was there. We lived together, but there were separate versions.

No way to say this is how it was. Facts that seem so carved in stone are printed in sand — a wind, a wash of rain changes the impression. No truth as such. I heard them argue back and forth, the truth taffy being pulled. Circumstances are what it comes down to, aggravating and mitigating. Some things will make the outcome of a trial worse, some will make it better. It all depends. If you tell about a troubled childhood, then you might earn sympathy for a man who's wrecked by flaws, but you might also prove the reason behind his guilt. Ought it be laid bare or not? Facts are a risk, honesty isn't justly wise. In a trial, sides of truth, versions are held up and the jury weighs them and determines their own vision of the way it was. They vote one way or another, and do the best they can by their convictions. They try to gather enough facts, enough truth to judge a man, to do him justice.

At the hearing, Cole's victims read statements about the pain and suffering he had caused them, caused their families. Tom Betts was there. And the store clerk he'd beaten with the bat, whose left arm now hung limp at his side. The clerk's mother spoke about her son, changes she'd seen in him since Cole had hurt him. That was the saddest part. The hardest was looking from them to Cole. My son sat with his head down, his face pale. He never looked up. Maybe it was for shame. He didn't want to have to see what he'd done to them, to their lives.

But I didn't look away, and I listened to every word they told about their torment. And I looked again at my boy I would always love, helpless not to. From the stand, the clerk's mother sought out my eyes, found me in the crowded courtroom to talk to. One mother to another. I wouldn't have needed to hear her story, how hard it was to not be able to do anything to make her son's arm useful again, she could only watch his suffering. How hard it was only to watch. I knew her in myself without she said anything. My son's clothes were hanging in his closet now, the moths making lace out of them. I opened the door more often than I should, put my cheek to the cloth. I would have told my story, told her about being sorry, and love, if anyone had given me a word to say.

Cole was condemned to death for killing the police officer while committing a felony, imprisoned at Riverbend Maximum Security Institution in Nashville. Appeals were launched right away, his case would go through the entire legal process in both state and federal courts at least once. It would take years. Came back to time again. In jails, Cole used to spend a lot of his time leaning against the bars of his cell, hanging his arms out through them as if they at least could get some freedom. But in mandatory segregation, in his single cell in unit 2, it was a solid steel door with just a narrow slit of a plexiglass window. All the doors in the pod were the same, no bars. His stayed closed. The door was painted blue on the outside, the color of summer sky. But the side Cole saw, inside it was black. He taped a map of the stars to the ceiling above his bed. He laid long hours staring at it, until it became almost real to him, almost the real night sky. He gazed at the stars, the arc of his cigarette still burning in the dark. I wondered what the stars did for him. Calmed him, I think, but maybe it was like staring at infinity, futures and futures. I wondered if he told himself the song, *When you wish upon a star, makes no difference who you are.*

Ivy is in her motel room, after everything she's been through with Cole, she's here. A date and time is set for Cole's execution, further legal appeals seem hopeless. Now it moves fast. After all those years — the penalty of death looming — it has shrunk down to days, less than a week. Everything condensed. It has come down to an exact hour, hands on a clock, held up at midnight. Ivy has come to say goodbye. She is not the person she was then, but she knows it's a slippery line of blood and tears between love and hate. She remembers hating loving my son. But she did love him.

I sit with her in her room, each of us on a single bed watching the news on the television. She is eating peaches for the pits. She likes Georgia Belle or Elberta peaches best, is saving the pits to carve into a first wives collection, beginning with Jackie O. She doesn't want to limit herself to presidents. She says it like a challenge to me but I don't see why she should, she can do what she wants. The peaches upset her stomach now that she is pregnant, carrying her sister's baby for her. She's nauseous most of the time. She won't just take the pits out of the peaches because that would be a waste. She says she's glad to be an artist even if it makes her sick. We both smile. I tell her she ought to get some sleep. Why not give me the peaches, I'll eat them while I watch a late movie in my room? I don't tell her I don't plan on sleeping, I couldn't, I don't want to dream.

Before I leave, I give her something, a present for the baby. She unwraps the paper and lifts out the tiny knitted bonnet. "You have to keep their heads warm," I tell her, "at the beginning. Babies need so much, it's hard to know where to start. Maybe you could pass it on to your sister." The way she holds the bonnet then, feeling the soft cotton wool between her fingers as though it was something precious, not wanting to put it down, I wonder how it will be for her when the baby comes and she has to give it up. I don't tell Ivy that lately all I've been doing is knitting baby bonnets. I have a suitcase full, pale yellow as buttercups. Babies need so much, how to give it to them?

In the morning, I meet Cole's lawyer and we drive to the Governor's office together. Now I am my son's last hope. After all these years, I can speak when it's almost too late, when there's little chance anything I say will make a difference. Still. I am the last one to stand and plead for my son's life. And the Governor is the last person who can change Cole's fate, grant him clemency and he won't be put to death but spend his life in prison. I will speak, the Governor will give me his time and decide. He has never commuted a death sentence, public pressure is against it, politically it would not be the best choice for him. I know. Still. If he shows mercy, my son will be able to walk outside his cell without his hands and legs chained.

The Governor's press aide leads me into his office. I ask to go in alone, and Cole's lawyer nods, takes a seat outside to wait for me. The Governor is standing behind his desk with his legal aide and a PR person on either side of him. He shakes my hand warmly. Two security men stand at the back of the room. We sit down and he pours me a glass of water from a jug on his desk. "Don't be nervous," he tells me. "Speak from your heart."

My head swirls. Suddenly I don't know where to begin. I take a deep breath. I tell him, "There was a tornado." Then I stop. I look at him, terrified. I don't know that I will be able to say anymore, but he nods. There was a tornado. "Nobody saw it coming," I say. "Children died. It was a natural disaster. But there's nothing natural about your children dying in front of you. I thought I was blessed when my son was born out of that destruction. I've spent years thinking about what I know and what I don't know. Always, understanding is hard. I've tried to look at moments. Study nature, how it is, the natural world. The fact of nature, what's born inside a child. The tornado caved in the roof of a church. That wasn't supposed to happen. A church should be safe. I don't know where is safe." I take a drink of water. My words are a rush, Niagara Falls pounding away its foundation, white water falling.

"I think about demons," I tell him. "Storms inside a man's head." I say it again. "Storms," to make sure he hears. "You can't see wind, but it will crush you flat, it doesn't care about children. You can't hold it. Like love. You can't stop it. Like being sorry. I have always loved my son," I say, and look at him.

He nods. Then he stands and shakes my hand again, ushers

me out into the lobby. My legs take me, but I'm lost, my head still swirling. I don't know what I said, what words were more important than others, which would weight the scale one way or tip it another. I am hopeful and full of regret all at once. The lawyer is sitting on a bench reading a paper from his briefcase, waiting for me. A secretary is talking on the phone. The sun is shining through the windows, as if the glass weren't a barrier. In an hour, the Governor lets us know he appreciated my comments but the sentence of death will be carried out as scheduled.

At the execution, the gurney will be in the shape of a cross. Cole will lay with his arms outstretched. From the death chamber he can see into the witness room. He will see me. I will say the Twenty-third Psalm to him as he is put to sleep. *He leadeth me beside the still waters. He restoreth my soul.* After long years of non-contact, I will be able to touch him. I will stroke his cheek, kiss his eyelids, his pretty long eyelashes. I will press my lips to his forehead. I will finally touch my son after he is dead.

When I leave the prison, I will drive to Harlin's house, tell him to pack his bags. He won't want to come with me, north to Canada. North to cold clear lakes, and pink granite, and dazzling auroras. He thinks he knows what it would be like from pictures and books. Still. I want him to see it with me.

I will tell him about the Birdman of Alcatraz. He was in prison for fifty-three years, from 1912. When he got off the Rock — he was being transferred to another prison — an airplane flew above him in the sky. The Birdman looked up. The guards felt sorry for him, it was on their faces. They asked if it was strange for him to see a plane, when there was no such thing when he was first put behind bars. It was that long ago. But instead the Birdman told them all about the plane. It was a Boeing 707, it weighed 247,000 pounds, cruised at 595 miles an hour. He knew more than they did. They couldn't believe it, he showed them.

"But Harlin," I will say, "him knowing about that plane and him being on it, flying through the clouds a free man, are two different stories." I hope he will decide to come with me.

I've spent my life wondering why Cole was born to me, how much was my fault, how much we just are who we are even before we come into this world. I hoped if I held up moments to the light, studied them like sparkling diamonds, sharp to cut glass, stars in a boy's eyes, I'd know why — something that ought to shine darkens to black. I know I loved Cole from the start, and then Ivy came along and loved him too. It wasn't a lack of love. When I leave the prison, Cole's spirit will already be borne on the wind to heaven. I hope heaven for him. A kinder wind at his death than was there at his birth. I hope that calm spirit wind will be gentle on my mind. I want the sky, a clean blue slate.

ACKNOWLEDGMENTS

The kindness, wisdom, and many tolerances of my family, friends, and neighbors have carried me on through the writing of this book. I thank them gratefully. I have been especially fortunate to be able to count on the insight and advice of Michael Wray, Stevenson Baker, Wallace King, Cynthia Holz, Michele Hoskin, Joan Whitman, my agent Anne McDermid, my eagle-eyed and true-hearted editor Iris Tupholme, Karen Hanson, Susan Thomas, and all the staff at HarperCollins. They are my anchors, essential.

I appreciate also the faith and support of Willeen Owen who is a remarkable woman and an inspiration, Sandra Owen-Peters, Julian Peters, Derrick Fulton, Daniel Richler, Patrick Crean whose literary vision is impeccable and whose care is legendary, Catherine Bush, Joseph Wray beloved and amazing to me, Steven Heighton, Lisa MacRae, Gail Backus, and the students I have had the privilege of working with whose talent and dedication impress and hearten me.

In Nashville, my friend Cathie Pelletier, whose words and friendship are poetry to me. Also Tom Viorikic, Carl Hileman, Steven Womack, Sharyn McCrumb.

Thank you Pam Hobbins, and Thomas Joplin at Riverbend

Maximum Security Institution for letting me see all I needed and ever wanted to see of death row. It was invaluable. Despite what I've written, though ninety-seven people are on death row in Tennessee, it remains the only state in the South not to have executed an inmate since 1960.

My gratitude to the Canada Council, the Ontario Arts Council, and the Toronto Arts Council for financial assistance.